THE *NEW YORK TIMES* BESTSELLING

WARM BODIES

"Gruesome yet poetic. . . . A paean to the power of storytelling. . . . The words Marion uses to describe his grim near-future are silken smooth. They slip through the mind's grasp easily, pleasurably, leaving hardly a hint of themselves in the images they evoke."

—*The Seattle Times*

"It's got the boarded-up strongholds and mob mentality of *Night of the Living Dead*—but also romance."

—*Time Out New York*

"*Warm Bodies* is a strange and unexpected treat. R is the thinking woman's zombie—though somewhat grey-skinned and monosyllabic, he could be the perfect boyfriend, if he could manage to refrain from eating you. This is a wonderful book, elegantly written, touching and fun, as delightful as a mouthful of fresh brains."

—Audrey Niffenegger, #1 *New York Times*
bestselling author of *The Time Traveler's Wife*

"Dark and funny."

—*Wired*

"Marion explores the meaning of humanity through R's journey towards personhood, a tale that gets grander in scale as his empathy builds and the book's true villains—cynicism, apathy, and status quo—are revea[led] . . . *Magazine*

"Isaac Marion has a great new voice that hooks you from page one and accomplishes the impossible: it makes you care about young zombie love. *Warm Bodies* is a terrific read."

—Josh Bazell, *New York Times* bestselling author of *Beat the Reaper*

"A jubilant story about two star-crossed lovers, one of them dead and hungry for more than love."

—Kirkus Reviews

"Marion is a disarming writer, ruefully humorous, knowingly cinematic in scope. This is a slacker-zombie novel with a heart."

—*The Guardian* (UK)

"*Warm Bodies* is a terrific book—a compelling literary fantasy which is also a strange and affecting pop-culture parable."

—Nick Harkaway, author of *The Gone-Away World*

"R does possess a certain winsome charm, and the upbeat ending will warm many hearts."

—*Publishers Weekly*

"A visually arresting, bleakly Ballardesque world . . . wryly playful, cinematic, and ultimately moving."

—*Time Out London*

"I never thought I could care so passionately for a zombie. Isaac Marion has created the most unexpected romantic lead I've ever encountered, and rewritten the entire concept of what it means to be a zombie in the process. This story stayed with me long after I was done reading it. I eagerly await his next book."

—Stephenie Meyer, #1 *New York Times* bestselling author of the Twilight saga

"A mesmerising evolution of a classic contemporary myth."

—Simon Pegg, *New York Times* bestselling author of *Nerd Do Well*

"Both tender and lacerating, this zombie novel has more to say about being alive than being dead. 'Love' is not a strong enough word for my feelings about this book."

—Maggie Stiefvater, author of the Shiver trilogy
and *Books of Faerie*

"Enormous fun."

—*Marie Claire* (UK)

"*Warm Bodies* is a terrific zombook. Whether you're warm-bodied or cold-bodied, snuggle up to it with the lights low and enjoy a dead-lightful combination of horror and romance."

—*Examiner.com*

"A captivating debut novel that is as romantic as it is terrifying. . . . Marion is an amazing storyteller who writes from his heart, or from his viscera, as the case may be."

—*SFScope*

"A unique and poignant story about life, love, and change. . . . Marion's writing style is straightforward, funny, and strong, just like his characters. . . . You can't help but be drawn into this postapocalyptic world and root for love and hope where none should exist."

—*Fresh Fiction*

"Thought provoking and highly original. . . . Imaginative characters and quirky dialogue make this a captivating read . . . that readers will devour."

—*Dark Faerie Tales*

"Has there been a more sympathetic monster since Frankenstein's?"

—*The Financial Times* (UK)

ALSO BY ISAAC MARION

Warm Bodies

THE NEW HUNGER

A WARM BODIES NOVELLA

ISAAC MARION

EMILY BESTLER BOOKS

—

ATRIA

NEW YORK   LONDON   TORONTO   SYDNEY   NEW DELHI

EMILY
BESTLER
BOOKS

ATRIA PAPERBACK
An Imprint of Simon & Schuster, Inc.
1230 Avenue of the Americas
New York, NY 10020

First Emily Bestler Books/Atria Paperback edition October 2015

EMILY BESTLER BOOKS / ATRIA PAPERBACK and colophon are trademarks of Simon & Schuster, Inc.

Lyrics from "Let Down" used by permission of Alfred Music Publishing Co. Inc. Words and music by Thomas Yorke, Jonathan Greenwood, Colin Greenwood, Edward O'Brien and Philip Selway. Copyright © 1997 Warner/Chappell Music Ltd. All rights in the US and Canada administered by WB Music Corp. All rights reserved.

Interior illustrations adapted by Isaac Marion from sources in the public domain.

For information about special discounts for bulk purchases, please contact Simon & Schuster Special Sales at 1-866-506-1949 or business@simonandschuster.com.

The Simon & Schuster Speakers Bureau can bring authors to your live event. For more information or to book an event, contact the Simon & Schuster Speakers Bureau at 1-866-248-3049 or visit our website at www.simonspeakers.com.

Manufactured in the United States of America

10   9   8   7   6   5   4   3   2   1

Library of Congress Cataloging-in-Publication Data is available.

ISBN 978-1-4767-9965-0
ISBN 978-1-4767-9970-4 (ebook)

For Jenae and Kevon.
Wherever you are, I hope you found good people.

The past speaks to us in a thousand voices, warning and comforting, animating and calling to action.

—Felix Adler

beginning

This is not the beginning.

The beginning is darkness and fire, microbes and worms—the very first of us, killing by the billions on their way up the ladder. There is little to learn from the beginning. We prefer the middle, where things are getting interesting.

Who are we? We are everyone. We are every thought and action. Time is just a filing system for the vastness of our Library, but we linger in the present with the unfinished books, watching them write themselves. The world is changing. The globe is bulging and straining, erupting and blazing with miracles, and we don't know what shape it will take when it cools. Even with all of history inside us, we don't know, and this is a little scary.

So we narrow our focus. We zoom in on a country, then a city, then the white rooftop of a stadium, where three young people are sitting on a blanket.

The sky is dark. They are the only ones awake for miles around. It's hard to catch a sunrise in the middle of summer—the sun barely sets before bouncing back up—but today the need to see beauty was urgent. They have seen too much ugliness. Their lives are smeared with it like blood and shit, so thick they can barely breathe, so today they're on the roof in the cold morning air, waiting for the sun to wash them.

Who are these people? Why do they interest us? They are not special—no one is—but there is something in them that draws our gaze. A short, pale girl full of strange dreams. A tall, dark girl with a promise carved on her heart. And a half-alive man whose head buzzes with voices, who talks to us and listens without knowing we exist.

We want them to know we exist. We want them to read our Library and share it with the world, because there is nothing sweeter than being known. But first we have to know them. We are books that read our readers, not a story but a conversation, and we open it with a question:

Who are you?

We circle around them, peering in the windows of their souls.

What's in there? Where did it come from? Show us and we'll show you.

Up and down the Library, from its bright ceiling to its black basement, pages begin to flutter.

THE NEW
HUNGER

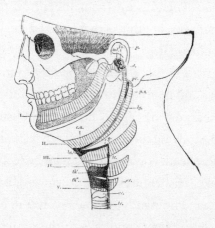

A DEAD MAN LIES near a river, and the forest watches him. Gold clouds drift across a warming pink sky. Crows dart through dark pines that hover over him like morbid onlookers. In the deep, wild grass, small living things creep around the dead man's face, eager to eat it and return it to the soil. Their faint clicks mingle with the rush of the wind and the screams of the birds and the roar of the river that will wash away his bones. Nature is hungry. It is ready to take back what the man stole from it by living.

But the dead man opens his eyes.

He stares at the sky. He feels an impulse: *move*. So he sits up. His eyes are open but he can't see anything. Just a blur that he doesn't know is a blur, because he has never seen clarity.

This is the world, he reasons. *The world is blurry.*

Hours pass. Then his eyes remember how to focus, and the world sharpens. He thinks that he liked the world better before he could see it.

Lying next to him is a woman. She is beautiful, her hair pale and silky and matted with blood, her blue eyes mirroring the sky, tears drying rapidly under the hot sun. The man tilts his head, studying the woman's lovely face and the bullet hole in her forehead. For a brief moment he feels a sensation he doesn't like. His features bend downward; his eyes sting. Then it fades and he stands up. The revolver in his hand slips through his limp fingers and falls to the ground. He starts walking.

The man notices that he is tall. Branches scrape his scalp and tangle in his matted mess of hair. The tall man notices other things, too. A leather chair floating in the river. A metal suitcase hanging from a branch. Four more bodies with holes in their heads, sprawled out limp in the grass. These ones are not beautiful. They are pale and spattered with black blood, regarding the sky with strange, metallic grey eyes. He feels another unpleasant sensation, and he kicks one of the bodies in the head. He kicks it again and again, until his shoe sinks into the putrid mess of its brain, and then he forgets why he's doing this and keeps walking.

The tall man does not know who he is. He does not know what he is or where he is, how he came here or why. His head is so empty it hurts; the vacuum of space is twisting it apart, so he forces a thought into it just to ease the pain:

Find someone.

He walks away from the blond woman. He walks away from the bodies. He walks away from the column of smoke rising out of the trees behind him.

Find another person.

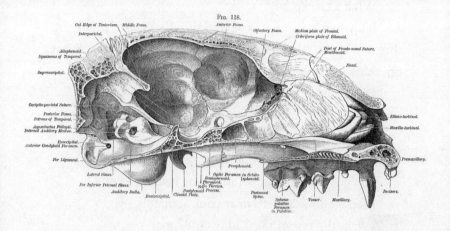

A GIRL AND HER BROTHER are walking in the city. Her brother breaks the silence.

"I know who you like."

"What?"

"I know who you like."

"No you don't."

"Yeah I do."

"I don't like anybody."

"Do too. And I know who it is."

Nora glances back at Addis, who is such a painfully slow walker she wants to put him on a leash and drag him.

"Okay, who do I like?"

"I'm not telling."

She laughs. "That's not how blackmail works, dumb-ass."

"What's blackmail?"

"It's when you know a secret about somebody and you threaten to tell people unless they do what you want. But it doesn't work if you don't say what you know."

"Oh. Okay, you like Evan."

Nora fights a surprised smile. The little shit's got eyes.

"You *do*!" Addis crows. "You like Evan!"

"Maybe," Nora says, looking straight ahead. "So what?"

"So I got you. And now I'm gonna blacknail you."

"Black*mail*. Okay, let's hear your demands."

"I want the rest of the Teddy Grahams."

"Deal. I don't like the chocolate ones."

"And you have to carry the water an extra day."

"Fine. But only because I *really* don't want anyone to know I like Evan."

"Yeah, because he's ugly."

"No, because he has a girlfriend."

"But he *is* ugly."

"I like ugly. Beauty is a trick."

Addis snorts. "No one likes ugly."

"I like you, don't I?" She reaches back and grabs a handful of his woolly hair, shakes his head around. He laughs and wrestles free. "Okay, so are we good here?" she says. "Do we have a deal?"

"One more."

"All right, but only one, so you better make it good."

Addis studies the pavement scrolling by under his feet. "I want us to look for Mom and Dad."

Nora walks in silence for a few sidewalk squares. "No deal."

"But I'm blackmailing you!"

"No deal."

"Then I'm gonna tell everyone you like Evan."

Nora stops walking. She cups her hands to her mouth and sucks in a deep breath. "Hey everyone! *I like Evan Kenerly!*"

Her voice echoes through long canyons of crumbled high-rises, gutted storefronts, melted glass and scorched concrete. It rolls down mossy streets and bounces off piles of rusted cars, frightening crows out of a copse of alders that sprouts through the roof of an Urban Outfitters.

Her brother scowls at her, betrayed, but Nora is tired of this. "We were just playing a game, Addy. Evan's probably dead by now."

She starts walking again. Addis hangs back a moment, then follows, still scowling. "You're mean," he says.

"Yeah, maybe. But I'm nicer than Mom and Dad."

They walk in silence for five minutes before Addis looks up from his gloomy study of the sidewalk. "So what *are* we looking for?"

Nora shrugs. "Good people. There are good people out there."

"Are you sure?"

"There's got to be one or two."

"Do I still get the cookies?"

She stops and raises her eyes skyward, letting out a slow sigh. She slips off her backpack and pulls out the bag of Teddy Grahams, hands it to her brother. He shoves the last two into his mouth and Nora studies him as he chews furiously. He's getting thinner. A seven-year-old's face should be round, not sharp. It shouldn't have the angular planes of a fashion model. She can see the exhaustion in his dark eyes, creeping in around the sadness.

"Let's crash," she says. "I'm tired."

Addis beams, revealing white teeth smeared black with cookie gunk.

They set up camp in a law firm lobby, wrapped in the single wool blanket they share between them, the marble floor softened with chair cushions. The last red rays of the sunset leak through the revolving door and crawl across the floor, then abruptly vanish, severed by the rooftops.

"Can we make a fire?" Addis whimpers, although the night is warm.

"In the morning."

"But it's scary in here."

Nora can't argue with that. The building's steel skeleton creaks and groans as the day's warmth dissipates, and she can hear the ghostly rustle of paperwork in a nearby office, brought to life by a breeze whistling through a broken window. But it's a law firm. A place utterly useless to the new world, and thus invisible to scavengers. One threat out of a hundred checked off her list—she will sleep one percent better.

She pulls the flashlight out of her pack and squeezes its handle a few times until the bulb begins to glow, then gives it to Addis. He hugs it to his chest like a talisman.

"Good night, Adderall," she says.

14

"Good night, Norwhale."

Even with the powerful protection of a two-watt bulb against the creeping jungle of night, he still sounds scared. And she can still hear his stomach, growling louder than any monsters that may lurk in the dark.

Nora reaches across their makeshift bed and squeezes her brother's hand, marveling at its softness. Wondering how mankind survived as long as it did with hands this soft.

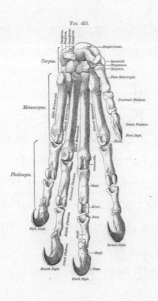

Fɪɢ. 453.

For the first time in weeks, Julie Grigio is having a dream that's not a nightmare. She is sitting on a blanket on a high white rooftop, gazing into a sky full of airplanes. There are hundreds of them, gleaming against the sky like a swarm of butterflies, writing letters on the blue with their contrails. She is watching these planes next to someone who loves her, and she knows with warm certainty that everything will be okay. That there is nothing in the world worth fearing.

Then she wakes up. She opens her eyes and blinks the world into focus. The tiny cage of the SUV's cabin surrounds her, spacious for a vehicle, suffocating for a home.

"Mom?" she blurts before she's fully conscious, a reflex born from years of bad nights and cold-sweat awakenings.

Her mother twists around in the front seat and gives her a gentle smile. "Morning, honey. Sleep okay?"

Julie nods, rubbing crust out of her eyes. "Where are we?"

"Getting close," her father answers without taking his eyes off the road. The silver Chevy Tahoe cruises at freeway speeds down a narrow suburban street called Boundary Road. It used to terrify her, watching mailboxes and stop signs streak past her window, imagining neighborhood dogs and cats thumping under their tires, but she's getting used to it. She knows the faster they drive, the sooner they'll find their new home.

"Are you excited?" her mother asks.

Julie nods.

"What are you excited about?"

"Everything."

"Like what? What do you miss most about real cities?"

Julie thinks for a moment. "School?"

"We'll find you a great school."

"My friends."

Her mother hesitates, struggling to maintain her smile. "You'll make new friends. What else?"

"Will they have libraries?"

"Sure. Maybe no librarians, but the books should still be there."

"What about restaurants?"

"God, I hope so. I'd kill for a cheeseburger."

Julie's father clears his throat. "Audrey . . ."

"What else?" her mother continues, ignoring him. "Art

galleries? I bet we could find somewhere to show your paintings—"

"Audrey."

She doesn't look away from Julie but she stops talking. "What."

"The Almanac said 'functioning government,' not 'thriving civilization.' "

"I know that."

"So you shouldn't be getting her hopes up."

Audrey Grigio smiles stiffly at her husband. "I don't think any of us are in danger of a hope overdose, John."

Julie's father keeps his eyes on the road and doesn't reply. Her mother turns back to her and tries to resume the daydream. "What else, Julie? Boys? I hear the boys are cute in Vancouver."

Julie wants to keep playing but the moment has died. "Maybe," she says, and looks out the window. Her mother opens her mouth to say more, then closes it and turns around to face the road.

Behind the perfect movie set of beige houses and green lawns, the border wall looms like a studio soundstage, making suspension of disbelief impossible. Big red maple leaves painted every hundred feet serve as stern reminders of who built this barrier, and who's keeping out whom. Julie loves her mother. She has high hopes for this new life in Canada. But she has seen more nightmares come true than dreams.

"There it is," her father announces. The truck hops a curb and descends into the border park lawn, tearing muddy grooves in the weedy grass. They drive past the booths where glorified mall cops once pretended to interrogate nervous college kids. *How long will you be staying? Are you carrying any alcohol? Where were you on September 11th?*

All that quaint border-crossing pageantry is over now. There is only one question still of interest to the gatekeepers of nations:

Are you infected?

The Tahoe rolls to a stop in front of the gate and Julie's father gets out. He approaches the black glass scanning window with his hands upraised. "Colonel John Grigio, US Army," he shouts. "Requesting immigration."

The wall is an impressive feat of construction for something built in such desperate times: thirty feet of reinforced concrete running from half a mile off the coast of Washington to somewhere deep in the Quebecois wilderness, and the whole length of it garnished with razor wire. The "gate" is just two tall slabs of galvanized steel, fitted flush to the concrete to make any prying or tampering impossible. Not that the automated guns mounted above it would allow the attempt.

The scanning window emits a few beeps. The guns twitch on their arm mounts. Then silence.

Julie's father glances around expectantly. "Colonel John Grigio, US Army," he repeats, "requesting immigration."

Silence.

"Hello!" He lowers his hands to his sides. "I have a wife and kid with me. We came from New York by way of the north and middle territories and have plenty of intel to share. Colonel John Grigio, requesting immigration!"

A red light blinks on behind the black glass, then fades. The twin surveillance cameras wobble briefly but remain pointed at random points in the grass, as if fascinated by some caterpillars.

"How old was that Almanac?" Julie whispers to her mother, gripping the seat to pull herself forward.

"Two months," her mother says, and the tightness in her voice pushes Julie's heart underwater.

"We have skills!" her father yells, his voice filling with an emotion that startles her. "My wife is a veterinarian. My daughter is combat trained. I was an O-6 colonel and commanded federal forces in twelve secession conflicts!"

He stands in front of the gate, waiting with apparent patience, but Julie can see his shoulders rising and falling dangerously. She realizes she is seeing a rare sight: a glimpse into her father's secret bunker. His hopes were as high as his wife's.

"Requesting immigration!" he roars savagely and hammers the butt of his pistol into the scanning window. It bounces pitifully off the bulletproof glass, but this action finally elicits a reaction. The red light blinks on again. The surveillance cameras wobble. A garbled electronic voice fills the air—*ARNING—SAULT RESPONSE—ETHAL FORCE*—and the guns begin spraying bullets.

Julie screams as geysers of dust erupt inches from her father's feet. He leaps backward and runs—not toward the truck but into the grass of the park. But the guns don't follow him. They spin on their arms, strafing the road, bending downward and bouncing bullets off the steel door itself, then they abruptly go limp, barrels bouncing against the concrete.

Julie's mother hops out of the car and runs to her husband's side. They both stare at the wall in shock.

FILE, it declares in its buzzing authoritarian baritone. *RESPONSE FILE CORRU—RETINA SCAN—AILED. REQUESTING RESPONSE FROM FEDERAL AUTHORIT—PASSWORD. PASSWOR—EQUIRED. WORK VISA. DUTY-FREE. APPLE MAGGOT.*

The guns rise.

Julie's parents jump into the Tahoe and her father slams it in reverse, lurching backward just as the guns spray another wild arc across the road. When they're out of range he pulls a sharp slide in the muddy grass, flipping the Tahoe around, and they all pause to catch their breath as Canada loses its mind. The guns have stopped spinning and are both pointed down at the same spot, diligently pounding bullets into the dirt.

"What the *fuck?*" Julie's mother says between gasps.

Julie digs through the duffel bag on the seat next to her and pulls out her father's sniper scope. She runs it along the top of the wall, past coil after coil of razor wire, scraps of clothing and the occasional bit of dried flesh. Then she sees an explanation, and her heart finishes drowning.

"Dad," she mumbles, handing him the scope. She points. He looks. He sees it. A uniformed arm dangling over the edge of the wall. Two helmets caught in the razor wire, one containing a head. And three city-sized plumes of smoke rising from somewhere beyond the wall.

Her father hands the scope back to her and drives calmly

toward the freeway, steering clear of the gun turrets that bristle from the Peace Arch. His face is flat, all traces of that unnerving lapse into passion now gone. For better or worse, he is himself again.

After five minutes of silence, her mother speaks, her voice as flat as her husband's face. "Where are we going."

"South."

Five more minutes.

"To where."

"Rosso's heard chatter about an enclave in South Cascadia. When we get in radio range we'll check in with him."

"What happened?" Julie asks in a small voice. Her only answer is the roar of the tires on the cracked pavement of I-5 South. There are dozens of answers for her to choose from, everything from anarchic uprising to foreign invasion to the newer, more exotic forms of annihilation that have recently graced the world, but the relevant portion of every answer is the same: Canada is gone. The land is still there, and maybe some of its people, but Canada the safe haven, the last vestige of North American civilization, the new place to call home— that Canada is as lost as Atlantis, sunk beneath the same tide of blood and hunger that drowned the home she fled.

Suddenly exhausted, she closes her eyes and slips into nightmares again. Graveyards rising out of the ocean. Her friends' corpses in the light of their burning school. Skeletons ripping open men's chests and crawling inside. She endures it patiently, waiting for the horror film to end and the theater to go dark, those precious few hours of blackout that are her only respite.

Julie Bastet Grigio has reasons to sleep darkly. Her life has seen little light. She is twelve years old but has a woman's weathered poise. Her abyss-blue eyes have a piercing focus that some adults find unsettling. Her mother ties her hair in a ponytail but Julie pulls it out, letting it fall into a loose mess of yellow and gold. She has fired a gun into a human head. She has watched a pile of bodies set alight. She has starved and thirsted, stolen food and given it away, and glimpsed the meaning of life by watching it end over and over. But she has just turned twelve. She likes horses. She has never kissed a boy.

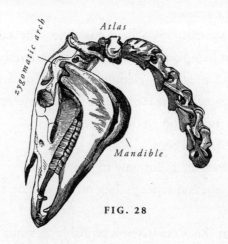

zygomatic arch

Atlas

Mandible

FIG. 28

WHAT CITY IS THIS? When did it die? And which of the endless selection of disasters killed it? If print news hadn't vanished years ago, Nora could find a paper blowing in the street and read the bold headlines declaring the end. Now she's left to wonder. Was it something quick and clean? Earthquakes, showers of space debris, freak tornados and rising tides? Or was it one of the threats that linger? Radiation. Viruses. People.

She knows that knowing wouldn't change anything. Death will introduce itself in its own time, and when she has shaken its hand and heard its offer, she will try her best to bargain with it.

"Can I go swimming?" Addis pleads.

"We don't know what's in there. It could be dangerous."

"It's the ocean!"

"Yeah, but not really."

They are standing on a new coastline. The ocean has grown tired of living on the beach and has moved to the city. Gentle waves lap against telephone poles. Pink and green anemones compete for real estate on parking meters. A barnacled BMW rocks lazily in the shifting tides.

"Pleeease?" Addis begs.

"You can wade in it. But only to your knees."

Addis whoops and starts pulling off his muddy, shredded Nikes.

"Keep your shoes on. There's probably all kinds of nasty stuff in there."

"But it's the ocean!"

"Shoes on."

He surrenders, rolls his jeans over his knees, and sloshes into the waves. Nora watches him long enough to decide he won't drown or be eaten by urban sharks, then pulls the filter out of her pack and kneels at the water's edge to fill her jug. She remembers a photo of her grandmother doing the same in some filthy Ethiopian river, and how it always made her glad she was born in America. She smiles darkly.

It took only eight feet to drown every port in the world. New York is a bayou. New Orleans is a reef. Whatever city this is, it's lucky to be sitting on a hill—the ocean has claimed only a few blocks. While her brother splashes and squeals, Nora scans the waterline for any trace of actual beach, some little patch of sand on the last remaining high ground. She remembers the feeling of sweaty toes digging into cool mud.

She remembers sprinting on the thin after-waves that slid over each other like sheets of glass. When she ran with the waves it looked like she wasn't moving. When she ran against them it looked like she was flying. She refuses to believe her brother will never know these things. Somewhere, they will find sand.

When she looks back at him he's in up to his neck, swimming.

"Addis Horace Greene!" she hisses. "Out, right now!"

"Brr!" he squeals as he dog-paddles past the post office, through soggy clusters of letters floating like lily pads. "It's cold!"

. . .

Nora is grateful that it's summer. The heat is unpleasant but it won't kill them. They can sleep in doorways or alleyways or in the middle of the street with nothing more than their tattered blanket to keep off the dew. She wonders how long her parents debated their decision. If they might have waited a few months for the weather to warm. She would like to believe in this tiny kindness, but she finds it hard.

"Do we have *anything* left to eat?" Addis asks, shivering in his wet jeans. "Even some crumbs?"

Nora digs through her backpack reflexively, but no miracle has taken place. No fishes or loaves have appeared. It contains the same flashlight, blanket, filter, and bottle it always has, nothing more. Not counting the Teddy Grahams, Addis's last meal was two days ago. Nora can't remember when hers was.

She turns in a circle, examining the surrounding city. All the grocery stores are long since gutted. She found their last few morsels in the kitchen of a homeless shelter—five cookies and half a can of peanuts—but that was an unlikely windfall. Actual restaurants are the lowest of low-hanging fruit and were probably stripped bare on this city's first day of anarchy. But something on the horizon catches her eye. She bunches her lips into a determined scowl.

"Come on," she says, grabbing her brother's hand.

They wriggle through a tangle of rebar from a bombed-out McDonalds, climb over a rusty mountain of stacked cars, and there it is, rising in the distant haze: a white Eiffel Tower with a UFO on top.

"What's that?" Addis asks.

"It's the Space Needle. I guess we're in Seattle."

"What's the Space Needle?"

"It's like . . . I don't know. A tourist thing."

"What's that round thing on the top? A space ship?"

"I think it's a restaurant."

"Does it go into space?"

"I wish."

"But it's the *Space* Needle."

"Sorry, Addy."

He frowns at the ground.

"But spaceships aren't full of food. A restaurant might be."

He raises his eyes, hopeful again. "Can we get up there?"

"I don't know. Let's go see if the power's still on."

It's eerier to be alone in a city that's lit up and functioning than in one that's a tomb. If everything were silent, one could almost pretend to be in nature. A forest. A meadow. Crickets and birdsong. But the corpse of civilization is as restless as the creatures that now roam the graveyards. It flickers and blinks. It buzzes to life.

When the first signs of the end came—a riot here, a secession there, a few too many wars to shrug off with "boys will be boys"—people started to prepare. Every major business installed generators, and when the oil derricks started pumping mud and the strategic reserves burned on a doomsday cult's altar, solar power suddenly didn't seem so whimsical. Even the brashest believers in America's invincibility shut their mouths and gazed at the horizon with a wide-eyed *oh shit* stare. Solar panels appeared everywhere, glittering blue on high-rise roofs and suburban lawns, nailed haphazardly onto billboards, blocking out the faces of grinning models like censorship bars.

By then it was too late for such baby steps, of course. But at least this last desperate effort will provide a few extra years of light for the next generation, before it too flickers out.

Nora gives her brother's hand a squeeze as they make their way toward the Space Needle. The sun is setting and the monument's lights are coming on one by one. The tip of the needle blinks steadily, a beacon for planes that will never leave the ground.

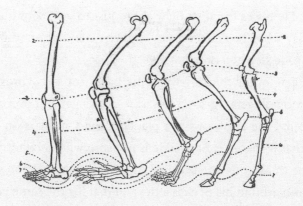

IN A REMOTE PATCH of forest that has never known human footprints, nature is witnessing a strange sight. A dead thing is moving. Crows circle it uncertainly. Rats sniff the air wafting from it, trying to settle the disagreement between their eyes and noses. But the tall man is unaware of his effect on the surrounding wildlife. He is busy learning how to walk.

This is a complex procedure, and the man is proud of his progress. His gait is far from graceful, but he has put appreciable distance between himself and the grisly scene of his birth. The black smoke is a far-off smudge, and he can no longer smell any trace of the blond woman's rotting body.

Right leg up, forward, down. Left leg up, body forward, right leg back, left leg down.

Repeat.

He knows he should be doing something with his arms as well but hasn't yet deduced what it could be. Waving? Flapping? He raises them straight ahead just to get them out of his way while he concentrates on the ancient art of ambulation. One step at a time.

A few other things have come back to him. Words for common objects—grass, trees, sky—and a general overview of reality. He knows what a planet is and that he is on one and that its name is Earth. He is not sure what a country is, but he thinks this one is called America. He knows the strip of cloth around his neck is a tie, and that it's the same color as the blood oozing from the bite on his leg, although that is rapidly darkening. The vacuum in his head is not as painful as it was, but there is another emptiness building in him. A hollow sensation that begins in his belly and creeps up into his mouth, pulling him forward like a horse's bit. *Where are we going?* he asks the emptiness. *Are you taking us to people?*

There is no answer.

As far as the tall man can tell, Earth is a world of grass and trees and water. He feels like it should be more beautiful than it is. The river is a sickly greenish brown. The sky is blue but not pretty. Too pale, almost grey. He remembers a sky that looked different—*sitting on the roof under noonday sun, listening to his father yell*—and rivers that were clean—*sinking to the bottom and holding his breath, wishing he never had to come up*—but the hollowness yanks him out of his reverie. He keeps walking.

The trees reach closer to the river until there is no more room to skirt around them, so he stops and regards the dark area where there are a lot of them together—*forest*. A smell of mildew and earthy rot emanates from it, stirring inexplicable terror in him—*Hole. Worms. Darkness. Sleep. Vast mouth and endless throat, down, down, down*—but he has no choice. He enters the forest.

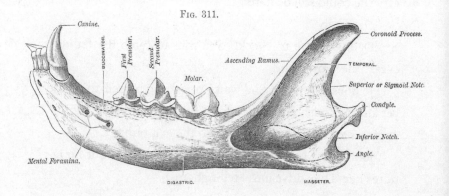

Fig. 311.

Canine. — Coronoid Process.

BUCCINATOR. First Premolar. Second Premolar.

Molar.

Ascending Ramus. —

TEMPORAL.

Superior or Sigmoid Notc.

Condyle.

Inferior Notch.

Angle.

Mental Foramina. —

DIGASTRIC.   MASSETER.

J ULIE WATCHES THE BACKS of her parents' heads, looming like stone idols in the front seats. No one has spoken in two hours. She watches the trees and empty fields become buildings, gas stations, college campuses. *Welcome to Bellingham,* an overpass mural declares, or used to declare before some cheery vandal sprayed the *B* into an *H* and crossed out *ingham.*

A spark of recognition goes off in her head and she lurches toward the front seats. "Hey! This is where Nikki lives!"

Her father glances at her in the mirror. "Who?"

"My pen pal? The deliveryman's niece?"

"The one who sent you a bottle of whiskey when you were ten?"

"Yes, Dad, that one. We have to stop!"

"Bellingham is exed. Nothing there to stop for."

"But I got a letter from her right before we left Omaha."

"That was almost a year ago."

"She could still be here."

"Not likely."

"Dad, we have to check!" She tries to catch her father's eyes. "She's my friend."

He doesn't answer. She waits, preparing herself to digest yet another wish denied. Then to her surprise, and without comment, her father swerves onto the exit ramp.

"John?" her mother says with some concern, but he ignores her. They drive into Hellingham.

• • •

The streets are cluttered with abandoned cars and the Tahoe weaves through them delicately like a show horse through barrels. Julie presses her face to the glass, scanning the windows of houses for any sign of movement. Most are boarded over. The ones that aren't boarded are broken. She sees movement in one, a sluggish shape lurching in the darkness of the living room, but she says nothing.

"Where does Nikki live?" her father asks in a genial, optimistic tone that draws a cold look from his wife.

"Downtown," Julie says quietly. "Holly Street."

They turn right on Holly, the thoroughfare Nikki always talked about in her letters. She made it sound like it was Mardi Gras every weekend, she and her college buddies gathering in riotous numbers, stumbling into the street and blocking traffic, laughing and singing, trying to forget the world that was crumbling around them. Julie had always wanted to see this street. To watch her friend drink and flirt and to learn firsthand how people keep living.

But Holly Street is paved with corpses. And other, less rotted corpses stagger through the mess like scavenging dogs, picking for scraps on the bones of their friends.

"What's the address?" her father queries loudly as the Tahoe runs over a body, his voice not quite masking the crunch.

Julie can't speak.

"Address?" he asks again as he swerves to hit a creature chewing on a girl's foot. Its brief grunt of surprise, the thumps and cracks as the SUV grinds over it . . .

"Twelve-twelve," she whispers.

Her mother is silent in the front seat, keeping her eyes carefully hidden from the mirror.

"Is this it?"

The Tahoe rolls to a stop, its tires crackling on gravel and glass. Julie rolls down her window and regards the old house. Front porch lined with moldy couches. Beer bottles and cigarette butts, muddy boot marks on the crooked walls . . . it was probably a ruin before the collapse, but it's a different kind now. Not the kind created by an excess of life. Not the result of seven young people crammed into a small house, desperate to enjoy themselves before the world they inherited burns up. The windows are empty holes lined with glass teeth. The front door is wide open and creaking in the breeze, and everything inside is dark.

"Nikki?" Julie manages to croak, despite the obvious. "Hello?"

Her father shakes his head and puts the truck in gear. Julie makes no objection as they pull away from the house. She says nothing as they head back to I-5.

"Was that really necessary, John?" her mother mutters.

"She needs to understand."

"Understand what? That all her friends are dead? That the world's a pile of shit? Christ."

His reply is the rev of the engine as he resumes their southward course.

Audrey Grigio twists her head around the seat to look at her daughter. "I'm sorry, honey."

Julie doesn't meet her gaze. She stares out the window as her friend's city recedes, giving way to pines and cedars, deep valleys and high mountains silhouetted against the browning sun. She wonders how many of her letters are moldering in the drop-off boxes. She wonders how long she's been writing to a ghost. She wonders what her friend's voice sounded like, and if she died in panic or acceptance, and if her twenty-one years had any effect on the relentless spinning of the world.

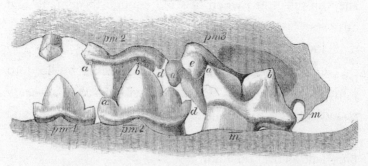

Fig. 337.

"WHAT ABOUT THESE?" Addis asks, holding up a pair of pruning shears.

"Too small."

He grabs a power drill. "This?"

"Nothing electric."

He picks up a nail-pull bar and holds it out. Nora considers it. "Nah. You need to be able to pierce a skull without much windup. Something with more focused weight."

The fluorescent lights buzz overhead as she and her brother browse the aisles of a hardware store in search of weapons. Their parents took the guns. Nora would like to believe it was for safety, that they didn't trust her not to shoot herself or Addis by mistake, but no. They've seen her shoot a militia sniper out of a seventh-story window, calmly aiming the family Glock in the dim morning light while they were still trying to untangle their blankets. She can find few excuses for her parents, and she wonders what she will tell Addis when he's old enough to demand real answers.

"How about *this*?"

He hefts a big, oak-handled axe. He presses his lips into a tough-guy scowl and takes a test swing, making a *whoosh* sound with his mouth. The axe slips out of his hands and crashes into a display of detergent bottles, spewing milky blue Tide all over the floor.

"It's the right idea," Nora giggles, "but maybe something a little more manageable."

She pulls two hatchets off the rack and hands one to Addis. He swings it, making the *whoosh* followed by a grisly *splat,* then grins at Nora. There is a savageness in this grin, a bloodlust that in any other era would have been patiently lectured out of him as he grew up. It scares Nora a little, but she says nothing. This is not any other era. This is now.

"These'll have to do," she says. "Now let's go find some food."

• • •

The Space Needle's lobby has been completely ransacked over the months or years, however long it's been since this particular city surrendered to the march of regress. All the T-shirts and hats are gone. All the mugs, sunglasses, and "Space Noodles" pasta. None of the looters took an interest in the snow globes, fridge magnets, or souvenir spoons.

Even the paperweights—which could potentially be used as bludgeons—are still here.

The lights in the lobby are broken out, but when Nora pushes the elevator button she hears machinery grinding into motion. Addis looks up at her, wriggling with excitement. Nora pulls her hatchet out of her backpack and waits.

The doors open with a polite *ding*. There is nothing inside that wants to kill them.

"Let me push it!" Addis shouts and begins scanning the rows of buttons.

"Not the top one, that's probably the view deck. There. That's the restaurant."

Addis pushes the button. The elevator soars upward, making Nora's knotted stomach groan in protest.

"Whoa . . . ," Addis gasps, pressing his face against the window as the city recedes below, spreading out to a hazy horizon of blue islands and waves. The disc at the top of the Space Needle rushes down and envelops them in darkness, then the doors open on the restaurant. Nora steps out and gives Addis a formal bow.

"Welcome to Sky City, sir. Do you have a reservation?"

He looks concerned. "What? What's a—"

She laughs and shoves him in the face. "Never mind. Come on."

She walks into the dining area and glances around, searching for the kitchen. Addis pauses at the edge of the disc's outer rim, which rotates slowly.

"It's *moving*!" he says.

"Yeah, I've heard about that. Cool, huh?"

"Are you *sure* it's not a spaceship?"

"Let's go look around. Maybe we'll find the cockpit."

Compared to most of the city below, the restaurant is in good shape. One table is missing its cloth and silverware and there's a wad of bloody bandages on one of the benches, but the place is otherwise unspoiled. No broken windows, no graffiti, no corpses. But they aren't here for the atmosphere.

They stand in front of the door of the walk-in freezer, paralyzed with suspense like game show contestants watching the wheel. Bankrupt or jackpot? Starve or keep going?

Nora pulls the door open. The freezer is full of food. Tubs of sliced vegetables, stacks of baguettes, bins stuffed with chicken breasts and steaks, a dozen sausage ropes hanging from the ceiling. And all of it is rotten. A room-temperature cornucopia of mold.

Addis's lips bunch and his brows squeeze down tight. He walks stiffly back into the kitchen and stands in a corner with his face to the wall, fists clenched at his sides.

Nora takes a deep breath and holds it, steps into the freezer and stares at the festering heaps of locally sourced organic ingredients. She thinks about those game show contestants, how they always took losing so well. They were college kids and single moms, hungry dropouts and desperate debt-cripples, and when the wheel informed them they'd just lost a life-changing sum of money and would go home with nothing, they laughed and sighed and clapped for their own demise. *Aw, darn!*

This is a different kind of show. The prize is not cash or a set of golf clubs; it's another day of life for Nora and her brother, and she is not about to lose politely.

She dives into the compost heap, knocking aside tubs of slimy asparagus, dumping bins of green chicken breasts, digging down through the mess as furry green sausages slap against her face. She gags from the smell and nearly vomits when her hand sinks into a turkey frothing with maggots. But at the bottom of it all, in a corner under some rat-gnawed bags of flour, she finds a box. She opens the box, and it's full of cans.

"Addis!" she shouts.

It's not a large box. Just three cans and a plastic tub: peeled potatoes, green beans, tofu, and some slightly rancid margarine. Not a life-changing win . . . but enough to pay off their hunger debts with a little left to spare.

She stands up with the box and finds Addis in the doorway, wide-eyed. "Guess what, Addy." She grins, savoring the novelty of what she's about to say. "We're going to have dinner tonight."

•   •   •

Pommes frites, fried in margarine. Green beans, sautéed in margarine. Margarine-infused tofu, with margarine sauce. It's the tastiest meal Nora has eaten since this impromptu family vacation began.

"You're a disaster," she says, watching Addis shovel handfuls of dripping potatoes into his mouth. He has wasted no time staining the white linen tablecloth and spilling all his water on the floor. "You're lucky you know the chef."

They have the best table in the house and the view is spectacular: all of Seattle spreads out for them through the floor-to-ceiling windows, fading east into the blue of the Cascades. Nora imagines bow-tied servers checking in on them, asking if they've saved room for dessert. She has always wondered what crème brûlée tastes like.

"These fries are way better than the ones at that gas station," Addis says through a mouthful.

"Glad you think so. Healthier, too."

"Really?"

"Slightly."

"That's good."

Nora smiles. A few months ago, the word "healthy" would have made him spit out his food. It's a bittersweet thing to see him finally valuing nutrition.

"Do you think they have music?" he wonders.

"I don't know if that's a good idea."

"Why?"

"If someone comes up the elevator, we might not hear them."

"So? They'll hear us and then they can have dinner with us."

"Addis . . ."

"What?"

Nora glances around. Addis watches her.

"Fine. Let me go check."

She makes a quick circuit of the restaurant, looking for the stereo controls but looking even harder for any signs that they're not alone. Those bandages. The blood is brown; they're at least a day or two old. She finds no other traces, so when she finds the stereo, plugged into some cleanup crewman's battered iPod, she spins through its playlists with a certain thrill, hoping to find something they can both enjoy.

"Billie Holiday?" she yells at Addis.

"Boring!"

"The Beatles?"

"They suck!"

"You little shit," she laughs. "I'm putting it on shuffle."

She presses play without looking and walks back to the table. Some soft piano begins, then a high, whispery voice layered with fragile harmonies.

"What's this?" Addis says, wrinkling his nose.

"Sounds like Sigur Rós."

"Why do you always listen to *old* music!" Addis groans.

"This isn't that old."

"It's like a million years old."

Nora sighs and flicks one of Addis's spilled green beans onto his shirt. A glint comes into his eye. He picks up a fry.

"No," Nora snaps, pointing her fork at him. "We are absolutely not food-fighting with this meal. Put it down."

Addis hesitates, sizing up her resolve.

"Sir," she says in cop-voice, "I need you to put the fry down immediately."

He pops it in his mouth. Nora nods and eats some tofu. They smile at each other as they chew.

The restaurant moves so slowly it's barely perceptible, but Nora notices they've made half a revolution since they arrived. The Cascade Mountains have been replaced by Puget Sound, pink and red, set ablaze by the setting sun. In the evening dimness, with the buildings all just silhouettes, the city looks perfectly normal. Many of the downtown high-rises are dark, but a few still have power, their tiny windows blinking on and off like Christmas lights. She watches her brother shoving fries into his mouth and somehow getting them in his hair, and she wonders where she's taking him. When they spend a whole day walking, where are they walking to? She has been avoiding this thought, but here it is again, insistent: she has no idea. She has no destination, or even a direction. She is making them walk because motion is the only plan she has. Because stillness is death.

Addis is looking out the window now, following her gaze. Her focus shifts to their reflections in the glass, ghostly faces surrounded by constellations of ceiling lights, and she is struck again by how different they are. He is tiny even for his age; Nora is already taller than her mother. His skin is dark like their father's; hers is a shade more Irish. Her hair is a briar of loose coils; his is a tightly woven nest that floats over his head collecting leaves, cobwebs, French fries. It's in desperate need of grease, so dry she could probably snap a chunk off in her fingers. His skin, too, so ashy he almost looks dead. It hits her suddenly how fragile he is. How constantly vulnerable. She doubted her ability to be a mother even before the end of the world. How is she going to do it now?

"Nora?"

He is looking at her uneasily. She wonders what her face has been doing for the last few minutes. She blinks away the beginnings of a tear.

"I need to go to the bathroom," she says, and stands up. The music has shifted to something modern, one of those new pop songs Addis and his friends used to listen to back in DC. It murmurs and clangs, slow and dark, the singer's androgynous voice doubled note for note by a mournful viola. It gives her goose bumps, and she makes a note to skip it on her way back. She never thought she'd be out of touch with youth culture by age sixteen. The darkness came so abruptly her tastes never had a chance to adjust, and now it all just scares her. She retreats into the past, to the records Auntie Shirley used to play while they built Legos in the living room. Some Ella or Billie or Frank would be nice right now, despite Addis's protests. There are worse feelings than boredom.

She pushes into the women's restroom and leans against the sink, fighting for composure. She looks in the mirror at her tired red eyes. She sees a large mound in the corner of the room, heaving slowly under a tablecloth.

. . .

"Addis, get your stuff."

"What?"

"We're leaving."

"But I'm not done eat—"

"Addis!"

He looks up at her, startled.

"Get your stuff."

Addis grabs his NPR tote bag and stuffs his hatchet into it next to a few bags of leftover food. Nora takes his hand and marches toward the elevator.

"What's going on?"

"There's something in the bathroom."

"Something?"

"Something or someone."

"Someone bad?"

"I don't know. It doesn't matter."

"But what if it's someone good?"

"Doesn't matter."

She drags her brother into the elevator and presses the lobby button. The elevator drops, pushing stomach bile into her throat.

"But I thought that's why we're walking around! I thought we're trying to find people who can help us."

"This person can't help us."

"How do you know?"

"Because they're lying on the floor under a bloody table-cloth."

"Are they hurt?"

"At least."

"Then shouldn't we help *them*?"

Nora pauses. She looks at her brother. It's a strange feeling, being judged by a child. He's seven years old; where the hell did he get a moral compass? Certainly not from his parents. Not even from her. She supposes there must be people in the world who stick to their principles, who always do the right thing, but they are few and far between, especially now. Where does a child get an idea as unnatural as goodness?

The elevator reaches the bottom. Addis watches Nora hopefully. She sighs and presses the restaurant's floor. They ascend.

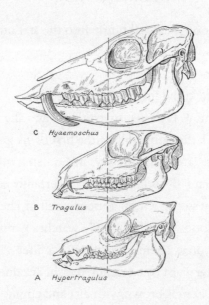

C   *Hyaemoschus*

B   *Tragulus*

A   *Hypertragulus*

THE SILVER TAHOE is low on gas. Julie can hear her father muttering about it every few minutes, scanning the surrounding landscape for likely filling stations. Eventually, on some obscure cue, he takes an exit into what appears to be a primeval forest. There are no signs advertising food or gas or civilization of any kind, but after a few miles a tiny truck stop appears, halfway hidden in the trees. Most of the city stations are drained dry. To find gas or anything else of value anymore, they have to look where no one else would. They have to turn logic backward and trust intuition, a skill Julie was surprised to find in Colonel John Grigio's stern repertoire.

"Does Dad have super smell?" she asks her mother as they

watch him hook the hand pump into the station's diesel reservoir.

"What?"

"How'd he know there was gas out here?"

"I don't know. He's just smart that way." She watches her husband work the pump, filling the first of six gas cans. "You have to appreciate that," she says in a quieter voice that Julie can barely hear. "If nothing else, he's certainly capable."

The sickly sweet, rotten apricot smell of chemically preserved fuel floods the air, and Julie watches her mother press a fold of her dress against her nose as a filter. A *white* dress, pulled in at the waist by a bright red sash. She doesn't seem to care that the hem is brown with dirt and engine grease, that there are small rips all over it revealing bare skin. The dress is pretty, so she wears it. Julie loves her for that, even though she herself is wearing work jeans and a grey T-shirt.

"I have to pee," Julie announces and hops out of the car.

"Not alone. I'll go with you."

"I'm twelve, Mom."

"You're veal." She grabs her Ruger 9mm off the dash and gets out of the truck. Julie rolls her eyes and walks around the back of the station with her mother in tow. She drops her jeans, her mother hikes her dress, and they crouch in the bushes.

"Remember those wine parties you and Dad used to throw?" Julie says.

"Sure."

"I wish we could have one now. I'm old enough to have a whole glass, right?"

"I'd say so. Don't know about your dad, though."

"I'll talk him into it."

Her mother smiles. "Maybe we can do something when we find the enclave. A housewarming party."

Julie watches her urine pool around her work boots. She browses the decades of graffiti scratched and sprayed onto the station's wall.

Big Dick Tim was here

Tim sux big dick

God still loves us!

God loves himself

~~NEVER~~ GIVE UP

"I want to get wasted," Julie mutters.

Her mother laughs.

Julie wipes with a leaf and buttons her jeans. A dead thorn branch catches on her mother's dress and pulls away with her when she stands. Her husband is waiting around the corner and he watches her tug at the branch until it finally rips free, tearing another hole in the bodice.

"You need some real clothes," he says. "We're not out for a picnic."

"Fuck off, John," she says cheerfully and brushes past him.

"By the time we get to the enclave you're going to be wearing a bikini."

"The better to seduce their leader."

They drive back to the freeway in brittle silence, and Julie thinks about wine parties. She thinks about their old house. She thinks about the day she found out her father used to have a band, and how her mother played his album for her and she laughed even though it was good, because how else could she react to the revelation that her father was human?

She peers into the passing trees, searching for wildlife. Birds, deer, something stupid and innocent that she can pretend to be for a while. Surely creatures that simple know how to be happy.

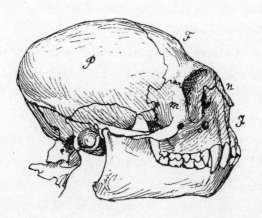

T HE TALL MAN is in pain.

The feeling that began in his stomach has now spread through his entire body and somehow beyond it. It radiates out from him like a cloud of ghosts, countless hands clutching at the air, reaching out for . . . something. He wishes he knew what it wanted, but it's a mindless brute. It lashes him onward with unintelligible grunts of need.

In some distant compartment of his mind, he is aware that the forest is beautiful. Despite the darkness and the musty tomb smell, there is a silence and softness that he finds comforting. He runs his hands along mossy tree trunks as he passes, enjoying their texture. *Like wool*, he thinks. *Like blankets. Her skin was—*

Something shifts. He can still feel the moss but it has been reduced to information: *Soft. Cool. Damp.* He no longer understands why he is wasting energy touching a tree, so he drops his hands and walks faster.

He is in a forest. He is surrounded by trees. He is wearing a tie the color his blood used to be, and slacks the color his blood is now. He is tall and thin but strong for his build—he surprises himself by snapping a branch as thick as his wrist. He carries it for a while like a club, because the forest is dark and he has seen creatures that aren't like him lurking in the shadows. Things that walk on four legs, covered in soft stuff like moss—fur—*wolves*. The forest is full of wolves, which he remembers are dangerous, and he feels afraid. But after a few hours the fear fades; he loses interest in the branch and tosses it aside.

It is becoming harder for him to maintain interest in anything but the hollowness. He is aware that tools and weapons might help him get what he wants, but what does he want? The hollowness seems to know, but it can't be bothered to explain. It pulses and pounds with one vague agenda, reflexively vetoing all other initiatives, even ones that might help it achieve its goals—such as carrying a weapon. The tall man will get no help from these impulses. He must decipher himself by himself.

He thinks about the wolves. He understands that they are not like him and that they want to hurt him. Maybe he wants to hurt them too. Maybe that's what he wants. Maybe creatures that are not like each other are supposed to hurt each other to find out which one is stronger, so that the stronger one can take the things it wants. A competition. A game. *War! Sex! Football!*

His eyes widen with these sudden bursts of insight. He is happy that he is remembering things. Perhaps soon he will have enough information to do whatever the brute in his belly is demanding.

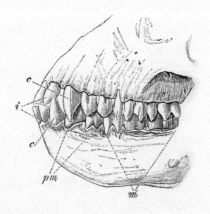

"**H**ELLO?"

The thing under the tablecloth continues to heave. The bloodstain in the middle of the cloth is bright red. Spreading.

"Hey. Are you alive?"

Nora stands in the bathroom doorway with her hatchet at the ready. Addis stands behind her, trembling despite all his noble ideals.

Nora takes a step inside.

"Listen. If you're still alive, you need to give me some kind of sign or we're gonna leave."

The cloth shifts slightly. A hand slides out from under it, palm down on the floor.

"Okay, that shows me you're still moving, but I need to know you're capital-L *Living*. So if you're not Dead, tap twice."

There is a long hesitation. The hand taps twice.

Addis grabs her shirt hem. She rubs his head.

"Okay," she says under her breath and approaches the heaving mound. Holding her hatchet high, ready to strike, she pulls the tablecloth away.

Addis hides his eyes behind his hands and starts whimpering.

The man under the cloth is a certified giant. At least six foot five, probably two hundred fifty pounds of the kind of hard bulk that looks like fat until it flexes. He is bald except for some light stubble on the sides of his head, which expands into a beard surrounding big, soft lips. But what Nora notices most is the gaping hole in his stomach, slowly saturating his white T-shirt. It appears to be a gunshot wound, but it has been sliced open with two crude, crisscrossing incisions. A steak knife lies on the floor next to him, as well as two bloody dinner forks. Someone was trying to perform surgery using dinnerware for a scalpel and clamps.

"Hey," she says. "What happened? Who shot you?"

The man's pale blue eyes fixate on her, dilating unsteadily. He opens his mouth, but all that comes out is a croak. He makes a vague waving motion and closes his eyes as if to say, *Doesn't matter.*

Nora lowers her voice. "Are they still here?"

He faintly shakes his head, eyes still closed.

"Who tried to take the bullet out? Is someone else with you?"

His eyes open. His hand moves like he's trying to point somewhere, but he can't summon the strength. He moves his lips on his next exhalation, and Nora hears the outline of a word, perhaps a name, but it's too faint. A ghost. He closes his eyes again. Tears glint in the corners.

Nora feels her stomach clenching. She stares at the hole in his belly, its ragged edges and dark center, a well of blood leading down into his inner depths. A wave of nausea sweeps through her; drops of perspiration pop out on her forehead.

"Listen," she says, "I'm not . . . I don't know how to . . ." She gingerly touches the edge of the wound. The sliced flaps of skin spread apart and she shudders. "I don't know what to do."

The man's head moves slightly. Nora would like to think it's a nod. That he understands. His eyes roll into his head, then return to hers.

Nora glances back at Addis. He is standing in the doorway, wringing his hands in front of his crotch and biting his lip.

He wasn't wrong. They did the right thing. But they shouldn't have.

She touches the man's fiery forehead. "I'm sorry."

He holds her gaze for a moment longer, then closes his eyes. A long, slow breath comes out of him and doesn't come back.

Nora stands up. "Addis, wait outside for a sec. I need to do something."

"Is he dead?"

"Yeah. Wait outside."

"Why?"

"Because I need to do something."

Addis looks at the hatchet clenched in her hand. His lips tremble and he backs out of the room.

Nora stands over the man, staring at his shiny bald head. She has never done this before. Her mind moves ahead to the sensations that will vibrate up her arms through the hatchet when it cracks the skull and sinks into the rubbery tissues inside. She raises the hatchet. She shuts her eyes. The toilet stall behind her creaks open and something groans and Nora screams and runs. She doesn't turn around to see what's there, she just runs. She grabs her brother's hand and drags him down the hall at a full sprint. Standing in the elevator pounding the "door close" button, she sees movement reflected in the restaurant's windows and hears a ragged howl, low and guttural but distinctly female. Then the doors slide shut, and they descend.

• • •

Addis is crying. Nora can't believe he still cries so easily after all the things they've been through. He cried when his mother dragged them out of bed and hid them in the bathroom while their father killed a looter with a crowbar. He cried when their apartment and the rest of Little Ethiopia went up in flames, his snot smearing against the window of the family Geo. He cried all the way from DC to Louisiana and then again when he saw New Orleans, yelling at his mother that the Bible said God would never again destroy the earth with a flood. He cried when his father said God is a liar.

Crying. Expelling grief from the body in the form of salt water. What's its purpose? How did it evolve, and why are humans the only creatures that do it? Nora wonders how many years it takes to dry up that messy urge.

"It's okay, Addy," she says as the elevator settles on the ground floor. "We're okay."

His sniffles don't completely subside until the Space Needle is hidden behind buildings far in the distance.

"What *was* that?" he finally asks as they trek north on Highway 99, the first words out of his mouth in thirty minutes.

"Guess," she says.

He doesn't.

They cross the Aurora Bridge just as the sun disappears behind the western mountains. Nora stops, although she knows she shouldn't. They are standing on a narrow sidewalk hundreds of feet above what was once a busy waterway, now a graveyard for sunken and sinking boats, million-dollar yachts floating on their sides, palaces for king crabs.

"Where are we going?" Addis asks.

"I'm not sure."

He pauses to think about this. "How far are we gonna have to walk?"

"I don't know. Probably a million miles."

He sags against the railing. "Can we find somewhere to sleep? I'm really tired."

Nora watches the last red glow of the sunset glitter on the water. Just before the sky goes completely dark, she catches movement out of the corner of her eye and glances back the way they came. On the edge of the hill, just before the bridge leaps out over the chasm, she sees a silhouette. A big silhouette of a big man, standing in the street and swaying slightly.

"Yeah," she mumbles. "Let's go."

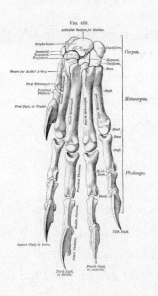

Fig. 460.

Articular Surface for Radius.

Scapho-lunar.
Scaphoid.
Trapezoid.
Trapezium.

Cuneiform.
Magnum.
Unciform.
Base.

Cuerpus.

Groove for Radial Artery.

First Metacarpal.
Proximal Phalanx.

Shaft.

First Digit, or Thumb.

Metacarpus.

Head.
Base.
Shaft.

Head Inter.

Phalanges.

Head.

Fifth Digit.

Second Digit, or Index.

Third Digit, or Middle.

Fourth Digit, or Annulus.

THE CLOUD OF HANDS has grown so large and strong it has begun to feel like an extra sense. Some warped hybrid of sight and smell and intuition. The tall man feels it reaching through the forest, its wispy fingers brushing through ferns and poking under rocks, seeking whatever it seeks. He struggles to ignore its constant moaning, which has begun to form words but is still too simple to be understood.

Get. Take. Fill.

He tries to distract himself by remembering more things. *What is your name?* Nothing. *How old are you?* Nothing. He hesitates before his next question. *Who was the woman by the river?* Something surges up from his core, a surprise heave of emotional vomit, but he gags it back down. *Her name was— the weight in your hand, the trigger—*

GUNS CAN KILL YOU! YOUR BRAIN IS IMPORTANT! DO NOT GET SHOT IN THE HEAD!

He is deeply relieved when this second voice interrupts. Its simple information is much easier to process than that terrifying eruption of feeling.

What you did—all the people you—

FIND OTHER THINGS LIKE YOU! THEY CAN HELP YOU GET THINGS YOU WANT!

And so a strange bartering session begins in his mind. He gives up the grief he felt upon seeing the woman and remembers what guns do and that he should avoid people who have them. He hands over his guilt and the desire to atone and receives the knowledge that he will be safer if he can find a group to join. It seems a very fair bargain.

A jolt ripples through the cloud of hands and his eyes snap open wide. His new sense has found something. The hands have reached very far, perhaps miles, and touched something that arouses them. They stretch off into the darkness of the woods, sending pulses of excitement back to him like Morse code.

Come. Follow. Take.

He obeys.

His muscles, which begin to cool and stiffen anytime he stands still, become supple again with whatever unknown energy drives them, and he walks at a brisk pace. The forest grows darker as he nears its heart. He glimpses strange things from the corner of his eyes: crystalline frogs and birds that glow, doors in the dirt and cyclones of bones, but he doesn't stop to wonder at these things. He has traded wonder for hunger. He follows the brute.

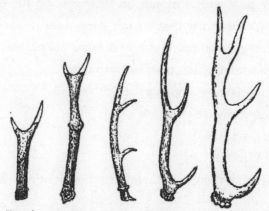

FIG. 61. FIG. 62. FIG. 63. FIG. 64. FIG. 65.

T HE SUN SETS faster than it used to. Nora is almost sure of this. It plummets like a glob of wax in a lava lamp, so rapidly she swears she can trace its motion, and she wonders if the earth has sped up. If perhaps somehow, all the bombs pummeling its crust have increased its spin. A ridiculous thought, but she still raises her walking pace. It's unfair to Addis's little legs, but he doesn't complain. He maintains a half run to keep up.

"Why don't we find a car?" he pants.

"Dad never showed me how to hotwire."

"What if somebody left their keys?"

"Those ones are probably all gone by now. But keep an eye out."

Addis abruptly stops and turns around. "What was that?"

Nora didn't actually hear it, so she feels okay saying, "Nothing. Probably boats knocking against each other. Come on."

They pass several motels on their way up the hill, but a bed isn't much use if you can't sleep, and she knows she won't tonight without a gun under her pillow. She pushes forward, scanning the storefront windows.

"Why aren't we stopping?" Addis says after keeping quiet for an impressive ten minutes.

"We need guns."

"But I'm *tired*."

"There are things out there that don't get tired. We need guns."

Addis sighs.

"Tell you what, A-D-D. If we find a lot of bullets, I'll let you shoot the next thing we need to shoot."

Addis smiles.

The neighborhood gets seedier as they move north. Pawn shops, smoke shops, dark alleys littered with condoms and syringes. This is encouraging. The "bad neighborhoods" of yesterday are the survival buffets of today, full of guns and drugs and all the other equipment necessary for living the low life. No neighborhood built for prosperity has any place in the new era—no one needs parks or cafés or fitness centers, much less schools or libraries. What's useful now is the infrastructure of the underworld, with its triple-bolted doors and barred windows, its hidden passages and plentiful supplies of vice. The slums and ghettos had the right idea all along. They were just ahead of their time.

"There!" Addis says, pointing at a storefront.

Nora stops and stares at it. A lovingly painted plywood sign, declaring in thousand-point font:

GUNS

She chuckles to herself. She almost walked past it.

• • •

Naturally, a cache this obvious has been thoroughly looted, but they search anyway. The display cases are empty, the ammo boxes are gone. There are more than a few puddles of dried blood on the floor, but no bodies. Whoever made this mess was careless. Everyone living in these times knows the most important rule of conservation: if you have to kill someone, make sure they stay dead. It may be a losing battle, the math may be against the Living, but diligence in this one area will at least slow down the spread of the plague. Responsible murder is the new recycling.

"This is the worst gun store ever," Addis says, scanning row after empty row.

"Pretend you're a looter. What places would you check last?"

"What are looters like?"

"I don't know, hungry? Scared?"

"Okay. That's easy."

"So you run into this place, you're hungry and scared, maybe you shoot some people . . . what do you do next?"

"Well . . ." A little smile blooms on his face as he gets into character. Nora realizes this is inappropriate make-believe to play with a seven-year-old, and for a moment she feels bad. But only a moment.

Addis runs around the store aiming an invisible pistol,

making *blam* sounds near all the blood pools and taking little grabs at the empty shelves. Then he turns to deliver his findings.

"I'd grab all the ones off the shelves first. Then the stuff in the cases. All the stuff that's right in front, 'cause I'd be scared to go into any back rooms or corners."

"Well I already checked the back room . . ."

"What if I was the owner of the shop?" His eyes widen with inspiration. "I bet I'd be even more scared then!"

"Okay, what if you were the owner?"

"I'd put guns in secret spots all over the store. So I could grab one no matter where I was."

Nora checks the cash register. Its drawer is open, empty. She checks the shelves under it. Empty.

"But if there was lots of shooting all the time," Addis continues like a scientist explaining his breakthrough theorem, "I'd probably be hiding on the *floor* a lot."

Nora shrugs and lies down on the floor behind the cash register, playing along. "Oh shit," she laughs. She grabs the Colt .45 taped to the cabinet molding and jumps up, aiming it at an imaginary target.

"Blam," she says.

Addis grins with huge, Christmas-morning eyes.

Nora checks the magazine. Full.

"I love you, Addis Greene," she says. "Let's go find somewhere to sleep."

. . .

When choosing their lodging, they ignore all the feeble enticements on the billboards. Fragmented advertisements with letters either missing or added by vandals.

CLEAN & QUI T
FREE INTERNmEnT
MONTHLY RA p ES

They base their choice solely on the thickness of the window bars.

Not wanting to damage their room's lock, Nora kicks in the office door instead, finds the key for the room farthest from the street, and enters the civilized way. Once inside, she locks the doorknob, latches the chain, hooks the hook, turns the deadbolt, the mortise, and the night latch.

This is a good motel.

A scan of the room brings a grim smile to her face. Peeling beige wallpaper. Dark orange carpet with wall-to-wall stains. Teal bedspread with a pink floral pattern. She tries the light switch but isn't surprised when nothing happens. Businesses in areas like this probably only bought gas generators, leaving the solar and hydrogen to the downtown folk. As a general rule, she doesn't expect to find electricity anywhere she can't find art galleries.

The moment she feels satisfied with the room's security, a wave of exhaustion washes over her. She plops down on the bed next to Addis and stares out the window into the darkness. After a while she feels Addis looking at her. She senses another round of questions building in him.

"What, Addy," she mumbles.

He doesn't answer. She notices a slight tremble in his chin.

"What's wrong?" she asks more gently.

"Mom and Dad . . . ," he says. "Where did they go?"

Her lips press into a thin line. "I don't know."

"Why aren't we looking for them?"

She hesitates, but she's too tired to protect him anymore. She lets it out in a breath. "Because they're not looking for us."

Addis's eyes focus on something far away. Nora braces herself, hoping he's still young enough to accept this and move on the way he does with a skinned knee or a bee sting. A good, hard cry, then back to playing, though the pain is still there.

"They're mean," he mumbles, glowering at the sheets.

Nora takes a deep breath. "Yeah, they are. But Addy?" She puts a hand on his shoulder. "It doesn't matter."

"Why not?"

"Because Mom and Dad are just people. Same as Auntie Shirley, Evan, anyone. Just because they *made* us doesn't mean they *are* us. They're mean and stupid and we're smart and cool, and we don't have to let what they do decide how we feel."

He looks at the floor, doesn't answer.

Nora raises an eyebrow at him. "At least . . . *I'm* smart and cool. Aren't you smart and cool?"

He lets out a heavy sigh. "Yeah."

"I thought so."

"I'm super smart and super cool."

"I knew it." She raises a palm. He slaps it weakly. "You ready for bed?"

Instead of answering, he crawls under the covers and curls into a ball with his back to her. Five minutes later, he's snoring. She sits there for a while, watching his breaths rise and fall under that hideous teal blanket. How much longer will simple logic and guidance-counselor pep talks be able to numb his wounds? Or hers, for that matter?

She slips under the blankets and stares at the mildewed ceiling. Despite her urgent exhaustion, her eyes won't close. Then sometime around midnight, she glances out the window and sees a man watching her through the bars.

For Addis's sake she stifles her scream. Biting her lip, her whole body shaking, she gets up and swipes the curtains shut. She stands there a moment, just breathing. She checks all the locks and turns in a slow circle, making sure there are no other doors or possible access points to the room. There aren't. And the door, in addition to its six different locks, has steel hinges as thick as her thumb. The owner of this motel must have been an avid reader of the signs of the times. The room is a vault.

Clutching the Colt, she pulls the curtains back for one last peek. The man is still there. His eyes, now pewter grey instead of sky blue, slowly track over to meet hers. Other than the desaturation of his irises and skin, he hasn't changed physically. He hasn't begun to rot. But it's astonishing how different he looks. He's not quite empty, his eyes still show a dim light of awareness, but whoever he was before, he is no longer. His face fits him like a cheap Halloween mask.

Nora knows she should shoot him right now, tell Addis the bang was just another of his nightmares and soothe him back to sleep, but she decides to leave it till morning. The man *could* throw rocks through the window, maybe shove a piece of wood through the bars if he's unusually motivated, but there really isn't much he can do to hurt them through those narrow gaps. And she has to admit, violence seems to be the last thing on his mind, if he has one anymore. He's just standing there, hands limp at his sides, looking at her. If she had to take a guess at reading his expression, she would say he looks . . . lost.

She shuts the curtain and climbs back in bed. She doesn't put the gun under her pillow as planned. She keeps it tight in her hand, safety off, polished steel cold against her thigh.

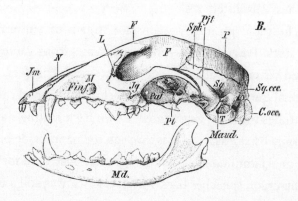

JULIE WATCHES THE SUN change from a fierce point of light to a sad orange blob that sags against the horizon like rotting fruit. She shivers when it disappears, imagining evil eyes snapping open in the trees surrounding the Tahoe, hungry mouths hissing *at last*. She knows this is stupid; her fear of the dark makes her feel like a child instead of a strong and capable twelve-year-old. There are monsters in the dark, of course, plenty of them. But there are just as many in the light.

Everything is going to be fine, the rich baritone on the truck's radio assures her. *The dark is always darkest before the brightness. Embrace your inner—Avoid major highways during militia activity. Stay in your homes until assistance arrives—Seahawks lead the Broncos forty-three to eight with three minutes on the clock . . .*

"For the love of God, John," her mother says. "Turn that shit off."

"You'd rather sit here in dead silence all night?"

"Yes! Absolutely yes."

The radio mumbles a constant stream of cultural non sequiturs. Fragments of sports broadcasts from games that ended years ago, ads for long-forgotten blockbusters, inspirational quotes from popular self-help authors, and calming platitudes from the government's own hack writing staff. It's the only broadcast that cuts through the nationwide blanket of signal jamming, a placeholder station once used for state-of-the-union speeches back when America was still a union. The government skipped town in a hurry, and they forgot to turn off the radio.

This summer, hold on to your balls. . . . Dwayne Lee is—

"*Please*, John," Julie's mother says. "I'm about to slit my wrists."

He turns the volume down, but only slightly. Audrey sighs in exhaustion and leans against the window.

"We could talk," Julie offers.

"I think it's bedtime," her father announces, and pulls off into a deserted rest stop alongside I-5. He shuts off the engine and Audrey visibly relaxes when the radio's schizophrenic chatter goes silent.

Julie's legs are numb, so she gets out of the truck and paces around, stamping her feet to revive the nerves. Her father opens the rear doors and grabs his shotgun off the ceiling-mounted rack. The rack holds three weapons: a big Army-issue riot gun for him, an automatic twelve-gauge for his wife, and a twenty-gauge Mossberg Mini for his daughter, which he procured after noticing the bruises her big Remington was inflicting on her shoulder. He gave it to her after they had to leave Omaha, and she got to use it the very next day, when Denver didn't work out either.

"What are you doing?" she asks him.

"Perimeter check." He starts toward the rest stop bathrooms.

"Hey Dad?"

He stops, turns.

"Is Seattle exed?"

"It's still a question mark in the Almanac, but probably. DBC takes their sweet time assessing the bigger cities."

"Do you think we'll find any people there?"

"No."

Julie releases a low sigh that gets lost in the wind. Her father finishes checking the buildings and heads out into the evergreen blackness. Her mind suddenly recalls one of last night's dreams and begins to flood with images—a deep, murky hole lined with teeth, a voice from the bottom beckoning her father—so she retreats to the Tahoe and sits in the driver's seat next to her mother. Her stomach growls like the voice in the hole. She reaches around the seat for the bag of Carbtein, tears open one of the little foil packages, and pops a dusty white cube in her mouth.

"Hungry?" she asks her mother, offering her a cube as she attempts to chew the one in her mouth. Her mother stares at it like she's never seen one before. Like she hasn't been eating these nutrient-packed billiards chalks and little else for months. She scratches at the sunken brown spots on her neck and shakes her head. Julie forces herself to swallow the lump of gritty, astringent mortar, then slumps into her seat, relieved to have it over with. She begins to wonder what they'll do when that bag is empty, but she stops herself. The bag is half full. That's what matters tonight.

Her mother switches the radio on and quickly flips away from Fed FM, which is currently playing a selection from its ten-song playlist of lab-tested pop hits. She leaves it on one of the many frequencies of static and leans her seat back, lying with her arms folded, gazing at the ceiling.

"At least static doesn't have commercials," Julie says.

Her mother's lips curve just slightly. "I would love to hear a commercial. I'd listen to commercials all day if it meant there were people out there making and selling things."

"Even those suicide pill commercials?"

"Especially those."

Julie doesn't understand this comment but it creates a cold feeling in her chest. She looks away from her mother.

"Has your life gone on long after the thrill of living is gone?" her mother quotes with a bitter smirk. "Are the dreams in which you're dying the best you've ever had?"

Julie starts flipping through stations, looking for something to change the subject.

"Knock, knock, knock on Heaven's door, with Enditol. Because only the good die young."

Each station plays a different genre of static. There's the bass hum station, the harsh crackle station, and Julie's favorite, the classical white noise station. Someone out there could be broadcasting a world-changing message, a solution, a cure, and unless Julie's family drove within a dozen miles of the source, it would be chewed up and swallowed by the jammers. She is not expecting to find anything worth hearing, just some static jarring enough to distract her mother from her dark thoughts. But then she lands on 90.3, and her mother's smirk vanishes.

"Mom!" Julie squeals under her breath.

For the first time in 1,394 miles, there is music on the radio.

It's an oldie. Something from the late nineties, long before pop music began to resemble horror movie scores. Julie's mother is transfixed as it streams through a gap in the clouds of static.

Starting and then stopping . . . taking off and landing . . . the emptiest of feelings . . .

She watches the radio as if the singer is inside it. Her eyes begin to glisten.

Floors collapsing, falling . . . bouncing back and one day . . . I am gonna grow wings . . . a chemical reaction . . .

The song ends. A young woman's voice replaces it, soft and shaky between spasms of static.

This is KEXP, 90.3 Seattle, bringing you the perfect soundtrack for huddling with your loved ones waiting to die.

To Julie's surprise, her mother laughs. She wipes at her eyes and grins at her daughter.

If you've been listening for a while I apologize for the repetitiveness. We usually try to keep things diverse here, but our door's being battered down as I record this and I didn't have much time to put a playlist together. . . .

Her grin starts to stiffen.

But anyway, if you're hearing this it means they didn't break the equipment, so enjoy the loop for as long as the power lasts. Consider it the last mixtape from us to you before our big breakup. I'm sorry, Seattle. America. World. We knew it couldn't last.

Julie's mother hits the radio's off button and sinks back into her chair. Her smile is gone with no trace.

"Mom?" Julie says softly.

Her mother doesn't respond or react. Her damp eyes regard the ceiling, as blank as a corpse's. Julie feels horrible things crawling in her belly. She gets out of the truck.

Her father is still securing the area, marching around with his gun in position, all procedure and tactics. Her mother has told her stories of when they were both young and wild. How they met on an airplane while in line for the bathroom, how he stole her away from her friends at the airport and showed her around Brooklyn, how they holed up in his tiny apartment for days and played music and drank wine and talked philosophy and causes and things they wanted to fight for. She knows he changed when the world changed. Adapted to survive. And there is a small part of her—a tender, bleeding organ that's been battered and bruised for too many years—that's starting to envy him.

She wanders out toward the trees that surround the rest stop like an infinite void. She sticks her earbuds in and clicks play on an iPod she found on a dead girl somewhere in Pennsylvania. There is a song on this dented, cracked device that she reserves for moments like these, when she needs a reminder that there's still a world out there. That her family is not alone on a spinning ball of rock.

The song is called "For Hannah." She has never heard of the band and the song isn't especially good. What makes it her favorite is the date listed on the file. It's the most recent date she's seen on a song by at least three years. Everything else in her collection was released back when there were still remnants of a music industry, money to be made and goods to spend it on. She has come to believe that this song—a sappy little ballad strummed clumsily on an out-of-tune guitar—is the last song ever recorded in the sunset of civilization.

Can you hear me? it begins. *Look up. . . .*

She stands at the edge of the forest, listening to the indefensible beauty of the singer's tuneless tenor, and whispers the melody into the shadows.

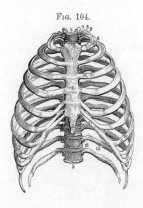

Fig. 104.

THE TALL MAN watches the girl. He stands absolutely still, staring at her through a gap in the bushes, and although she is so close he can see the freckles on her ears, she does not notice him.

What is she?

She is different from him. Smaller, softer, yes—he knows what a female is—but also something else. A fundamental contrast that has nothing to do with her physical shape. Something ephemeral that he can't explain.

The brute knows what it is. The brute is ecstatic about it. Its cloud of hands swarms around the girl, caressing her face, hissing into the man's mind:

This. This. This.

The man doesn't understand. He feels his hollowness lurching toward her, an angry prisoner flinging itself against

81

the walls of his belly, but he doesn't move. *What?* he asks. *What do you want?*

THIS.

His foot lifts off the ground. Left leg up, forward—

"Look up. . . . Look up. . . ."

He halts. A sound is coming out of the girl's mouth. He has heard similar sounds inside his head—*words*—but they are always short and blunt, devoid of tone, like the thud of heavy boots on asphalt. This is wondrously different.

"The clouds are parting . . . the window's open . . . time to grow a pair of wings . . ."

These are not just words. They bend and stretch and toy with pitch in a way that somehow elevates their meaning.

TAKE! the brute insists, growing furious. *FILL!*

Not yet, the man snaps back. *I want to try it . . .*

He opens his mouth and forces air through it. A harsh, phlegmy note honks out of him like an old bicycle horn. He wants to blush, but his blood is too congealed.

The girl's mouth clamps shut. She pulls out her earbuds and scans the trees with wide eyes.

"Dad . . . ?" she says, backing away.

The tall man starts to move toward her, but another person appears by her side, this one holding a gun.

"What's wrong?" this much bigger person says in a much different voice, harsher and less tonal, closer to the boot stomp of the tall man's thoughts.

"Nothing," the girl says. "I thought I heard something."

The sound of her special words—*singing*—rings in the tall man's head, gently teasing the tone-deaf idiot that lives there.

Come on, they seem to say. *Try a little harder.* The idiot in his head backs away from the girl's voice as he backs away from her father's gun.

He is glad he has information in his head instead of feel-ings. He is proud of himself for knowing what to do. The brute screams in protest as he creeps back into the forest, but he shoves it down. When he is a safe distance away, back in the smothering darkness of the woods, it finally surrenders. The cloud of hands goes limp, dejected, then slowly gathers itself and floats off in a new direction.

Soon, it growls at him, and although the man still isn't sure what he's agreeing to, he nods.

Soon.

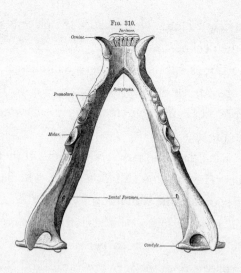

Fig. 310.

NORA IS IN Washington, DC, at the community center, doing practice volleys with her teammates.

Bump. Set. Spike.

She has managed to reduce everything to this. When a cult burns down her school, when a soldier corners her in a dark room, when she finds her parents on the floor with a pipe and powder, laughing and screaming like things born in Hell, she comes here. She puts on shorts. She hits the shiny white ball again and again and as long as she's here, the ball is all she has to think about. Keeping it aloft.

The community center is the one place that hasn't changed much in the upheaval. Its ping-pong table, its stained furniture, its snack machines and painfully earnest free condom dispensers—everything is still familiar, even the tired faces behind the help counter. Not because the place is somehow safe from the decline, but because it was already at the bottom before things fell. Nothing here will change until the bottom drops out. Until the president appears on TV to give the final good night and good luck, to cut everyone loose to scavenge in the dark.

"Girls!" a staff lady shouts over the sound of their squeaking sneakers. They all stop and look at her. The ball hits the floor. "You should come watch this."

They file into the lobby. All the staff people are crowded around the small TV in the corner of the room. Someone raises the volume until the speakers rattle, and Nora strains to make out the words through all the digital distortion and static.

Logic is no longer enough, says a man being interviewed in what appears to be a bomb shelter. *We have moved past the point where science alone can offer answers to our predicament. It's grown too large for that.*

"What's he talking about?" Nora whispers to the staff lady. The lady doesn't respond or move her eyes from the screen.

My question for you, Doctor, the host says, *is whether you felt this way yesterday, or if this is simply a reaction to today's news.*

Today's news? The doctor chuckles bitterly. *This isn't today's news. This is us finally acknowledging what's been happening all over the world for years.*

And when did you learn about it?

Last summer. A few days after my wife died in a car crash, when I woke up and looked out my bedroom window and saw her standing in the front yard, gnawing on a human head.

"What's he talking about?" Nora asks more loudly. Still no one looks at her. Signal interference spatters the screen with red pixels. She hears low laughter in the girls' restroom.

What is our reaction to that? How can we understand it? In the space of a few decades we've suffered nearly every catastrophe we ever imagined and now, with civilization already on the brink, we're given this. Our friends and families, all the casualties of all our conflicts, getting up again to keep the tragedy flowing. To consummate it.

The signal sputters and cuts off, detaching the two men's heads, scrambling their faces in a flurry of pixels and ear-piercing noise. Someone clicks the TV off and there is silence.

"What's he *talking* about?" Nora shouts, but no one answers her. Her friends stand with their backs to her, staring at the blank screen, unblinking. A warbling hum begins to fill the room.

She glances out the window and sees her baby brother playing alone in the mud of the playground. A gaunt black wolf stands behind him, drooling, grinning. Her teachers and teammates stare at the blank TV, ignoring her screams as the wolf's jaws stretch open.

• • •

"Nora!"

Her eyes snap open just in time to see Addis shutting the window curtain and dashing back to the bed, his eyes wide with panic.

"It's okay, Addy," she murmurs groggily.

"There's . . . there's a—"

"I know. He was there last night. He can't get in."

She climbs out of bed and approaches the window, fingering the Colt's trigger. She opens the curtain. The big man doesn't seem to have moved all night.

"Go away!" she shouts, her face mere inches from his. No reaction. She waves her hands in aggressive shooing motions. "Get the fuck out! Leave us alone!"

Nothing.

She raises the pistol and points it at his forehead.

Addis jams his hands against his ears. But before Nora can give her brother his next lesson on the brutality of modern life, the man pulls back. His expression remains blank, but he backs away from the window and steps aside like a gentleman holding a door for a lady. It unnerves Nora more than she would have expected.

"Get your stuff," she says to her brother, still aiming the gun.

"Aren't you gonna shoot him?"

"Not yet."

"Why?"

"Because he backed up."

"But isn't he a zombie?"

Nora hesitates before answering. "I don't know what he is. No one does."

She slips her backpack on and undoes the door locks, keeping her eyes and pistol trained on the man through the window. Addis huddles close behind her, gripping his hatchet.

"We're coming out!" she yells, having no idea if the man

still understands language. "You stay away from us or I'm shooting you!"

She opens the door a crack. He doesn't move. She opens it the rest of the way and steps out, keeping him firmly sighted. "All clear, Addis?"

Addis runs to each corner of the motel and peeks around, securing the perimeter like a seasoned police officer. His father taught him at least one thing well.

"All clear."

Nora walks backward toward him, not taking her eyes off the big man's dull silver gaze.

"Nora?" Addis says quietly.

"What."

"You should shoot him."

She glances back at her brother to make sure the voice really came from him.

"Auntie said we're not supposed to let them stay alive. If you don't kill him he's gonna kill someone else."

"I know what Auntie said." She keeps her sights on the center of the man's forehead. "And Dad said don't waste bullets on other people's problems."

"But Dad is mean."

Her teeth are grinding. The gun is getting slippery in her hands. The big man watches her calmly, standing a safe twenty feet away, arms hanging at his sides.

She doesn't want to shoot him.

She doesn't know what possible good it could do to spare his life, but she knows she wants to. Is it as simple as empathy? That uniquely human reluctance to kill? It can't be. She's killed two people since her fourteenth birthday. Yes, she did it in self-defense to protect her family, but does that really matter? Is the difference between killing with satisfaction and killing with horror nothing more than context?

"I can look away," Addis offers.

"What?"

"If you don't want to shoot him 'cause of me, I can look away when you do it."

"Addis, just shut up, okay?"

He shuts up. There is a long silence.

"Hey!" Nora shouts at the man. "You're infected, right? You're not just mute or sleepwalking or something? You're capital-D Dead?"

No response. As if she needs one. As if his skin, his eyes, and the gaping wound in his stomach weren't enough. She knows exactly what he is, but . . .

"Hey," she almost pleads, knowing she is talking to no one, nothing. "Can you understand me?"

He nods.

Nora gasps. Her gun lowers.

She hears the creak of a door behind her and whirls around. A naked woman is standing three feet from her face, skin grey and mottled and split open in places, head tilted to the side, a beard of brown blood running down her mouth and neck. Her jaw creaks open and she moans, a hollow sound of pain and hunger, and she lunges.

Nora is a good shot. She has excellent spatial awareness and eye-hand coordination, making her naturally talented with guns. But she is not a killer. She is not a war vet, she is not trained by the Army or National Guard or even local militias. The art of murder is not embedded in her muscle memory and she is not immune to shock. So when this drooling wreck of rotting flesh surges toward her, she doesn't calmly fire a round into its frontal lobe and walk away. She screams like a teenage girl and empties all seven rounds into its chest.

She doesn't have time to pull out her hatchet. The bullets slow the corpse about as much as paintballs. Its fingertips swipe for her face. She stumbles backward and trips, falls on her butt, kicks hard at the corpse's ankle and feels it snap like brittle plastic. The corpse topples onto its side and Nora scrambles to her feet, sprints to her brother and stands protectively in front of him while the corpse staggers upright. It takes two steps toward her with its loose, floppy foot dragging against the pavement, then stops, looks down at the broken foot, steps on it with the other, and heaves. Its foot tears off like a stubborn shoe. The corpse advances, stumping forward on its bare tibia like a peg leg.

Nora has seen all she can handle. Without premeditation or planning, she grabs Addis's wrist and runs back toward downtown Seattle, not because there is shelter or food or ammo there, but because it's downhill. She manages one final glance toward the motel. The Dead woman is giving slow pursuit, but the man hasn't moved. He stands where Nora left him, just watching her go.

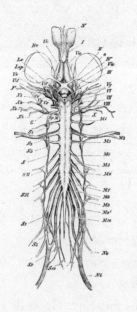

THE TALL MAN has been cheated. Some of the information he bartered for is false. He knows that he is in a North American forest and that there should be things like wolves and bears and deer in it but instead there are strange things that shouldn't be here or anywhere. Floating eyes and trees that breathe and snakes with silky blue fur. He does not know where to send his complaints. He does not know how he'll ever get a grasp on this world if it keeps changing.

He has been walking in the dark for six hours. His mind is losing what little rigidity it had, melting into mercury and oozing through the cracks. The brute in his belly is in a panic, screaming at him over and over, and he is growing weary of its ranting.

TAKE GET STEAL HAVE FILL

Shut up! he finally snaps. *I can't do it until you tell me what it is! So shut up!*

To his surprise, the brute shuts up. The man walks onward, his mind ringing in the sudden silence. And then, in a sour grumble, as if pried out of a pouting child, a specific imperative finally emerges:

Eat.

The man stops walking and slaps a palm over his face. That was it? *Eat?* He remembers eating. Eating is easy.

Why did you dance around it so long?

The brute is silent.

The man begins foraging. He finds a huckleberry bush and pops a handful of the plump red globes in his mouth. He bites down, expecting juicy sweetness—and feels the sensation of biting into a dead moth. The juice tastes like attic dust. The texture is dry and flaky, despite how the berries feel in his hands. He spits them out and stares with horror at the pulpy mess on his shirt.

The brute smirks.

He searches until he finds some wild mushrooms and shoves one in his mouth. Although he can feel its fleshy softness in his fingers, his mouth tells him he's crunching into a ball of dead wasps. He spits it out with a moan.

The brute laughs.

The cloud of hands mobilizes again, darting deeper into the forest, and a rich new scent pulses back to him through the cloud. *Blood. Flesh.* He follows it into a small clearing and discovers the source: a young deer hobbling through the underbrush, blood pouring from its claw-raked haunches.

This? he asks the brute, and the response is a mumbled, slightly sarcastic *maybe.*

The deer's dark, round eyes regard him with desperation. Part of him recoils from the impulses surging into his hands and teeth, but that part is no longer in charge. He seizes the deer and bites into its neck.

Blood pours down his throat. He rips out big chunks of meat and his mouth plays no tricks on him. The meat tastes like meat. The blood tastes like blood, salty and metallic. But when it hits his stomach, there is no spreading warmth of satiety. He drops the deer and stands up, waiting for it, but when his stomach finally responds, it's not the answer he expected. A dark rush of wrenching, twisting hunger knifes into him, as if he's suddenly minutes from starvation.

Eyes bulging, he leans over and vomits.

Wrong! the brute giggles into his ears. *Wrong wrong wrong.*

He vomits until it feels like his stomach will twist inside out, then stands over the deer gasping and shuddering. *What do you want? Tell me!*

Eat, the brute purrs, retreating back into the shadows, as if the answers to all questions are contained in this single word.

The cloud of hands drifts toward an opening in the trees, beckoning him with long, curling fingers, and he follows. He squints as he emerges from the dank woods into crisp air and blinding light. He is on a hill overlooking a valley, and there is something amazing in this valley. Towering rectangles of concrete and glass. A tangled web of streets winding through *houses* and *businesses* and *banks* and *bars*.

City.

All these words return to him at once, conjuring a wild spray of images. *People swarming in shopping malls, flashing plastic cards, putting paint on their faces and rings on their fingers. People sleeping in alleys, sticking bottles in their mouths and needles in their arms. People naked in beds, kissing. People naked in showers, crying. An old man in a tall building, grinning and sipping a drink as his soldiers fill the streets.*

THERE, the brute shouts, interrupting his daydream, and the images fade. *GO. TAKE. EAT.*

The cloud of hands surges down into the city like a squid on the hunt. With his head bowed, the man goes where he's led.

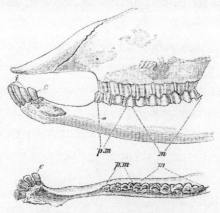

FIG. 235.—TEETH OF SHEEP (*Ovis aries*).

"ARE WE GOING BACK to the Space Needle?" Addis asks when the motel has vanished from sight and they have recovered some composure.

"No."

"Why are we going over this bridge again?"

"I don't know."

"You don't know?"

"Surprise. Big sister doesn't know everything."

Silence.

"Maybe we should go up there." He points east, toward a distant hill topped by three radio towers.

"Why?"

"I don't know."

"If you want to go places for no reason, just keep following me. You get to be our new leader when you come up with a plan."

"Maybe there's people up there. Look at all the houses."

Nora considers the plateau of colonial homes, balconies and roof decks, stunning water views. That must be where all Seattle's money used to go. Surely those estates have good enough security to keep out a few shambling corpses.

"Okay," Nora says, shrugging. "Let's go find Bill Gates's house."

"Who's Bill Gates?"

"A rich guy."

"What's 'rich' mean?"

Nora opens her mouth to answer, then chuckles, pondering the vocabulary of future generations.

"Nothing, Addy," she says. "Nothing much."

• • •

When they reach the bottom of the highway hill, she looks back to see how far they've come and notices two figures in the distance, cresting the peak. They are so far away they'd be invisible except that they're the only things in her field of vision that are moving. She can't make out any details of their faces or features, but one of them is much taller than the other and the short one is limping severely.

So they travel together on their little murder spree. Boney and Clyde. How cute.

"Those things are following us," Nora tells Addis as they exit the highway and start heading east, toward the trio of radio towers that tops the hill like a tiara. "We need to find more bullets."

"I'm really hungry," Addis says.

"Did you finish your leftovers?"

"Yeah."

"Check mine."

He unzips her backpack and digs around in it while Nora waits. He pulls out one small Ziploc of fried tofu.

Nora frowns at it. "Is that all I saved?"

"Yeah."

"God. What a fatty."

Addis opens it and squeezes a clump of tofu into his mouth. He offers the bag to her and she starts to take it, then looks at her brother's face. His cheekbones.

"You have it," she says. "I'm not hungry."

Her stomach chooses that moment to growl ferociously.

"Are too," Addis says.

"Okay I'm lying. But you're a growing boy and I'm a crusty old teenager. You eat it."

"Do you think there's food in those houses?"

"Probably. Hopefully."

He relents. He squeezes out another precious helping of tofu and cold margarine and they keep walking.

They pass a small Airstream trailer turned on its side, napkins and plastic forks spewed out into the street. A menu Sharpied onto its steel panels advertises grass-fed burgers on locally baked brioche, but the stench emanating from it advertises maggots.

"Food," Addis points out.

"All yours."

Addis sighs and shoves his face into the Ziploc, licking out the last of the tofu.

"We'll look for food as soon as we get safe," Nora says. "Bullets before burgers."

He gives her an accusatory glare that's somewhat undermined by the globs of margarine in his eyebrows. "Are you gonna kill them next time?"

"I'm at least gonna kill the lady one."

"Why not the man?"

"I don't know. I'll probably kill him too. But he's a little different."

"Because he didn't try to eat us?"

"Maybe."

"Why didn't he?"

Nora doesn't answer right away. She is in good shape, but the hill is steep and stealing her breath. "Remember when we stayed with Auntie Shirley on our way out here?"

He watches the pavement under his feet. "Yes."

"Remember how when she got bitten, she just stood in the kitchen all day, washing the dishes over and over?"

"Yes."

"And she didn't try to eat Mom until two days later?"

"Yes."

"Sometimes when people turn into . . . 'zombies' or whatever . . . it takes a while for them to figure out what they're supposed to do. Maybe their personalities don't disappear right away, so at first they're just confused, and they don't know who they are or what's happening to them."

Addis is quiet for a while, digesting this. "So why is that one following us?"

"I don't know. Maybe 'cause his girlfriend wants to eat us. Or maybe just 'cause I was the last person he saw before he died."

Addis smiles. "Maybe he likes you."

"Maybe the girl likes you."

His smile vanishes.

• • •

By the time they reach the hill's main thoroughfare, Broadway Avenue, the sun is on its way down. Nora realizes they must have slept a lot later than she intended. She can't remember if they ever actually slept the night before. The days of scheduled meals and bedtimes feel like ancient myths. She struggles to remember the color of her mother's eyes.

They have entered a neighborhood that looks like it was once vibrant. Colorful storefronts with artful graffiti. Concert posters smothering every pole. Stylishly dressed corpses littering the streets, their scooped-out skulls brimming with rainwater.

Nora opens her mouth to tell Addis not to look at them, then realizes how absurd that is. She lets him quietly absorb the massacre, hoping he will somehow process all his horrible experiences without too much damage. That he will find a way to bathe in poison without letting it inside.

"Look!" he says, pointing toward the park on the other side of the street. "A swimming pool!"

The park is huge, and may once have been beautiful. Rolling hills of grass, now overgrown with weeds. Tall, elegant lampposts, now rusted. Its towering central fountain still produces a trickling stream where it must have once cascaded. The stream flows into a shallow pool less than a foot deep and fully accessible, none of the usual municipal railings and warnings, as if the city actually wanted people to play in it. Perhaps that headless couple holding hands in the bus stop used to sit on the benches here and watch their toddlers splash. Perhaps the college kids now feeding flies in the street used to get drunk and lie on their backs in this pool late at night, staring up at the stars, dreaming big dreams for themselves and each other. Nora is going to cry again. This fucking city. This fucking world. When will she harden to it?

She watches Addis peel off his shoes and socks, sweaty and filthy, spotted red from bleeding blisters. She watches him cool his feet in the algae-slimed water. She wants to join him—she is drenched in sweat and the summer air seems to ripple around her in little pulses—but she needs to stay ready. They are not safe.

"Oh! Fuck!" she gasps as Addis palms a huge spray of water down the front of her tank top. Addis almost falls over laughing.

"You *ass*hole!" she snaps, but she can't hide the smile on her face and Addis keeps laughing. She whips off her shoes and runs into the pool. Addis squeals and flees. Nora kicks water at his back as he hops out of the pool and sprints off into the shaggy grass.

"Hey!" Nora shouts. "Come back!"

"Can't catch me!" he giggles, and keeps running. Nora can see in the blurring speed of his feet that he's beyond her discipline. The feeling of running barefoot in a field of grass, tendons flexed tight, feet bouncing off the ground like springs. Like running on a beach.

She lets him run. He won't get far; he's going in circles. She tries not to think about the precious calories he's burning right now, maybe half a meal's worth. If they can't spare the energy for a brief sprint in a park, they might as well go join the corpses on Broadway.

She hears a low growl behind her. Not a groan, not a moan, not a shout or a war cry; none of the sounds she's used to hearing when something wants to kill her. Just a wet, rattling growl, like seashore rocks tumbling in the undertow. She turns around. A wolf is staring at her from under a nearby picnic table. Its eyes are ice blue. Like her mother's, she suddenly recalls.

It creeps slowly from under the table, eyes fixed on hers. A big Canadian timber wolf, thin and desperate, fur caked in mud, too weary to bother cleaning itself anymore. Another phantasm pulled from the dying world's fever dreams. Next will be dragons. Vampires. Demons. Ghosts. By the time the last human being—and there *will* be a last one, if only for a moment—realizes she is alone, the world will be nothing but the sum of her nightmares. Why should reality hold together with no minds left to force it?

Nora reaches for her hatchet and the wolf snarls as if it knows what a hatchet is. She glances right and sees Addis watching from a distant knoll, frozen with terror. She glances left and sees two more wolves slinking out from the trees near the edge of the park, leafy shadows stretching toward her as the sun sinks to the rooftops. Is this really how she's going to die? In a world with so many options for exit, wandering a ruined city with no food or medicine, surrounded by murderers and the hungry Dead, she's going to be killed by *wolves*?

And yet it fits. It's appropriate. If the Library of Congress can be destroyed by arson, the Louvre by mold and neglect, if all the cultural accomplishments of ten thousand years on this planet can be erased by a few decades of carelessness, why shouldn't this young American be devoured by wild animals in the middle of a city park?

Her bare feet dip into the warm water of the wading pool. Her back bumps against the fountain and she feels the thin trickle of regurgitated rainwater flowing down her spine. The wolves circle in, grinning.

The big man steps around the fountain and stands between her and the wolves. He groans loudly at them and it almost sounds like a word, but too hoarse to understand.

The nearest wolf leaps at him. It's no doubt aiming for his throat, but his throat is nearly six feet high so it gets a mouthful of his T-shirt instead. He grabs the animal and strangles it, or maybe breaks its neck—it takes only a few seconds for the wolf to go limp. The other two bite into his legs. He reaches down, seizes them by the scruff of the neck, and hammers their heads into the concrete until their yelps go quiet. Everything goes quiet. The big man, his bald head gleaming grey in the evening light, looks at the dead predators at his feet. He looks at Nora.

Nora runs.

"Did you *see* that?" Addis squeals when she comes to a stop next to him on the hill.

"Uh, no. I was watching the sunset."

"It was just like in *Beauty and the Beast!*"

The man picks up one of the wolves, sniffs it, tears off a leg and rips out a bite of the hot muscle, chews for a moment, then casually vomits into the fountain.

"Yeah . . ." Nora mumbles. "Kind of."

The man drops the wolf and looks up at Nora. There is plenty of distance between them and plenty of directions for her to run, so she stays put for now, waiting to see what he does. But he doesn't do anything. He just stands there, looking at her.

"Why'd you do that?" she shouts.

He doesn't react. She glances around, making sure his girlfriend can't spring any more horror-movie shock-entrances on her, maybe popping out of a garbage can this time since there are no doors nearby.

"Stop following us, okay? Leave us alone!"

A sound gurgles in his throat and passes through his lips. It's faint and he's far away, but this time she's sure it was a word.

"Did you hear him?" she asks Addis. "Did he just say something?"

Addis is squinting at the man, a queer expression on his face. "I think he said 'please.'"

"What the fuck . . . ," Nora mutters.

Out from behind the fountain, the man's girlfriend staggers into view, still visibly female but hard to call a woman anymore. Its shoulders are now bare bone with nearly transparent scraps of skin dangling off. Its internal organs have shrunk away from the bullet wounds in its chest; Nora can see the lovely sunset shining through the holes. Since she last encountered this creature just a few hours ago, its decay has advanced about a month.

"Leave us *alone!*" she screams, and drags Addis away from the park, her fingers white-knuckled on his wrist.

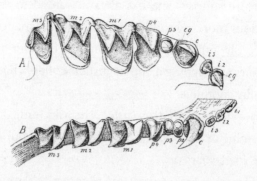

"Q!"

"Where?"

"Right there. 'Food next exit . . . Quiznos.' "

"Oh come on!"

"Stick that in your sandwich hole."

"I hate you, Mom."

Julie and her mother are playing the Alphabet Game. It is significantly harder without any passing license plates to read. They haven't seen another car on the road since Idaho, and that one rammed them into the median and disgorged two men who thought they'd found a nice little family to rob. That game of Alphabet ended with Julie and her mother wiping blood off the Tahoe's beige leather upholstery. She hopes this one will end with her being the first to spot the Seattle Zoo.

As always, she awoke to the hum of the tires and the seat belt cutting into her neck. Her father gets up at an hour that's only technically morning and usually has them on the road well before sunrise. She has always wanted to witness his mysterious morning routine but has never managed to wake up for it. She imagines him perusing old editions of the *New York Times* and sipping a cup of instant coffee while cleaning the family shotguns.

"How close are we to Seattle?" she asks him.

"Coming up on Burlington, so about two hours more unless the road clears up."

The freeway has been getting progressively rougher since Bellingham. Huge potholes, scattered debris, and the occasional scorched wreck of a vehicle, either blown up in a crash or burned by the Fire Church's "Ardents." The Tahoe has been steadily losing speed as they weave through the mess.

"What's the Almanac say about Burlington?" Julie asks. "Exed, right?"

"Last month's said there were still a few communes and markets functioning. Small towns last longer than cities sometimes."

"Why?"

"Not enough resources to attract militias and not enough Living to attract the Dead. If they're small enough, they get left alone."

"Why don't we live in a small town then?"

He looks over at his wife and smiles slightly. "Audrey?"

"Your dad thinks we should," she says. "What do you think, Julie? Should we move to a place that's too boring for zombies?"

"There are worse things than boredom," her husband counters.

"I'm not convinced of that."

He stares at her for a moment. He cocks his head. "What do you want, Audrey?" Anger simmers beneath his perplexity. "What is it you'd like us to do?"

Audrey leans back in her seat like she's settling in for a speech.

"You want to go back to Brooklyn? You want to work for the Axiom Group, help them claim the country? You want to clean their toilets and rub their feet while I go out and shoot little boys for a strong new America?"

"No, John," Audrey sighs.

"Then maybe you want to join one of the militias? The Brooklyn Bulldogs are probably wiped out by now. Bronx United's going to get shot in the back while they're fighting the Queens Kings. The Wall Street Traitors have a chance, but it's a pretty close match across the board . . ."

"John."

"I'm thinking it'll keep going till they've all killed each other or the floods force them off the island, but if you're tired of driving, we can—"

"John!"

He slams on the brakes; Julie's face smacks into the front seat as the Tahoe screeches to a stop. Stunned, she feels her nose to see if it's bleeding, then reluctantly follows her parents' gaze.

They have just crested a hill, and directly in front of them is a police spike strip. In front of the strip is a wall of wrecked cars that extends across all eight lanes of the freeway. And beyond the wall, stretching across a wide, green valley of overgrown farm fields, is what appears to be a war zone. What was once a shopping district has been reduced to a plain of pockmarked asphalt. The gutted, scorched interiors of big-box retailers are visible through gaping holes in their walls. The only vehicles in the parking lots are tanks, some with their turrets blown off, some lying on their sides, treads hanging like entrails; some marked *Army,* some spray-painted with the logos of various militias. And behind all this, as a perfectly hellish backdrop: the concrete skeletons of buildings engulfed in white flames of Fire Church phosphorous, left to burn for days as a warning. A monument. Or whatever their muddled message may be.

"Why?" Julie asks in a very small voice, unable to be more specific. There is, of course, no answer.

Her father grabs his shotgun and steps out of the truck, slipping into the hyper-alert posture of a soldier on perimeter check. Julie can't see anything moving down in the valley. It could have been deserted weeks ago and set ablaze recently by passing Ardents for a little morning devotional. She's hoping it's as empty as it looks.

"John," her mother calls to her father's back. "Let's just go around. We can take the back roads till I-5 clears up."

He doesn't answer. Julie can see in the set of his jaw and the animal blankness in his eyes that he didn't even hear her. He's in procedure mode. He will scout the area and ascertain possible threats before making any further decisions.

"John!"

He climbs into the bed of a pickup and pulls out his scope, begins scanning the smoldering valley below. Julie's mother sighs and grabs her gun. "Stay here," she tells Julie, locking the doors as she climbs out.

Julie watches her mother approach her father, her irritation visible in the stiffness of her stride. She watches them argue, their voices not quite audible through the window. Then she sees movement in her periphery and her window shatters. A man's arm reaches through and pulls the door open. She manages to grab her shotgun out of the ceiling rack just as two hands clamp around her ankles and yank her out of the truck. Her head hits the dirt hard and her vision swims. She sees a man's face hovering over her—not a man. A boy. Just a few years older than her. Fourteen or fifteen. His beautiful brown eyes are wild with desperation. His black hair is matted and filthy. The knife in his hand is crusted with dried blood.

Julie shoots him in the chest.

The world moves very slowly as she drags herself upright, clinging to the side of the truck. She is distantly aware of her parents shooting the boy's parents, who were emerging from a van with guns drawn and firing—she even notices the blood oozing from a graze on her father's thigh. But mostly, she notices the boy dying on the ground in front of her.

"Jesus Christ," she hears her mother muttering. Her parents are standing next to her now. She doesn't look at them. She looks at the boy, listens to his last breath leaking out of him, a slow hiss like a popped tire.

The three of them stand in silence for a moment. Then Julie's father bends down and picks up her gun—she doesn't remember dropping it. He places it in her hands.

"Are you serious?" Her mother's eyes are ice picks boring into her father's. "Are you fucking serious, John?"

"It's her third kill and we can't keep hiding this part from her. She needs to face it."

The boy's eyes begin to vibrate. Their color drains.

"She's *twelve years old*! She doesn't need to face this yet!"

"This is the world, Audrey. She knows that as well as we do."

Julie's mother shakes her head in disbelief. A wet, sloppy breath attempts to inflate the boy's punctured chest. Fixing her husband with a murderous glare, she steps toward the boy and starts to raise her pistol—then yelps as the boy's face vanishes in a spray of blood.

The valley reverberates with thunder. Audrey Grigio stares openmouthed at her daughter, and at the ghost of smoke creeping out of her daughter's shotgun.

Julie hops into the truck and snaps the gun into the rack. She fastens her seat belt and stares ahead with hollow eyes, waiting to leave.

Silently, her parents climb into the front seats. Her father drives into the grassy median to get around the blockade, working his way through the edge of the war zone to reach the residential side streets, which will be slower than the freeway but marginally safer.

"Hey Mom," Julie says.

"Yes honey."

Her mother's voice is faint and shaky. Julie hopes her own sounds stronger. She points at the markings on a destroyed tank, the American flag's red and blue scorched grey but the word "Army" still visible. "Found an 'R.'"

Fig. 195.

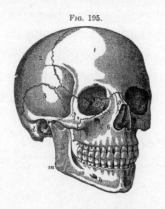

Despite everything he's traded away, the tall man still feels a faint sense of awe as he wanders through the city. These towering structures, this elaborate urban circulatory system . . . whatever sort of creature he is, he can tell by the shape of the doors and stairs and benches that this was all designed for bodies like his, and this pleases him. He must have some value if something this magnificent was built for him. The wolves have fast legs and sharp teeth but they don't have *cities*. He is excited to learn more about what he is— what he's called and what he's here for. Surely it's something wonderful.

The cloud of hands has not wavered since he arrived here, so he doesn't worry about getting lost. Each smoky tendril stretches off in the same direction, sending faint pulses of sensation back to him. A strange sort of smell that bypasses his nose and saturates his whole body. Floral sweetness spiked with sharp, electrical bitterness, like a lavender bush struck by lightning. But he finds it hard to enjoy this perfume when his body is collapsing from the inside out. Whatever energy drives his muscles is almost gone, and he can feel his cells beginning to shrivel up like raisins. The gentle hill he's climbing may prove an insurmountable summit.

How much farther? he asks the brute.

The brute ignores him.

Are we almost there?

Nothing.

How about now?

EAT, the brute snaps, then resumes its silence.

The tall man sulks as he staggers up the hill. Finally, the cruel incline levels out into a long, flat boulevard. He instinctively glances at the street sign but finds no information there. The symbols on it blur and spin and fail to register in his brain.

I can't read.

This thought surprises him, as he is not even sure what reading is. But what surprises him even more is the feeling that comes with it.

Loss.

What did he lose? What did he have? For reasons he can't explain, his enthusiasm for learning his nature dims.

His foot strikes something and he stumbles. He falls to the pavement and lands with his face inches from a round thing that looks like a face but has empty holes where eyes and a nose should be. He pulls himself upright and regards the long, spindly object attached to it—a body. The object is a body, brown and dry and withered. There are more like it all over the street. The cloud of hands pokes at them, mumbling something that's probably *eat*, then loses interest and floats off into the city without comment. But the man is intrigued. The bodies resemble him in shape, but like the ones by the river there is a fundamental difference that goes beyond the condition of their flesh. It's the same chasm that separated him from the girl in the woods, but yawning in the opposite direction.

An insight begins to bubble in his head.

Dead.

The bodies are *dead* and the girl is . . . *alive.*

He tilts his head and frowns. *Then what am I?*

A pulse ripples through the cloud of hands. It has found something.

Eat? the man prompts.

No answer. The brute is silent, pensive, as if studying a puzzle. What could possibly hold the attention of that drooling monomaniac? The man increases his pace, stepping over heap after rotted heap.

• • •

The sun is nearly set, bathing the bodies in a warm orange glow that makes them look slightly less inert. He can almost imagine them standing up and dusting themselves off, groaning and chasing after him, but he knows that's absurd. He knows what *dead* means now. It means gone forever. Lost. Irretrievable.

He sees a familiar shape ahead and feels a rush of happiness when he realizes what it is. A *person*. Not a body, not an object in the street waiting to become dirt—an actual person, like him. A man, to be specific, even taller than him and also big, a bearded, bald giant in a white T-shirt. He is just standing alone in the street, his eyes on the pavement, swaying slightly.

The tall man approaches the big man with quick, clumsy strides, tripping over corpses, bumping into cars, making no attempt at stealth, but the big man doesn't look up. His face is almost entirely blank, with just a faint trace of . . . an emotion . . . something bad maybe, but never mind; the tall man is too excited to focus on decoding emotional cues right now. He stops in front of the man and stands there, both of them swaying, but the big man still doesn't look up.

A trembling spasm begins to form in the back of the tall man's throat. He is going to speak.

He is going to say "hi."

"Hhh . . ." he says, managing only this throaty hiss.

The big man doesn't react.

"Hhh . . . hhh . . . *hi*." He feels profoundly satisfied. He has just greeted another person.

The big man's eyes slide up to meet his, and the tall man begins to notice things. The big man's eyes are silvery grey. The same grey that stared up at him as he kicked the corpse by the river over and over, filled with some desperate rage that seems utterly foreign to him now. The big man's skin is also grey, the same grey as the tall man's. And there is a gaping wound in his barrel-like belly, visible through the bloody hole in his shirt.

An insight:

The big man is dead.

And yet . . .

The brute studies this man intently. The cloud of hands pokes and prods at him like a doctor. Whatever the scent is that they've been following, that electric lavender perfume, it's completely absent from this man. But there is *something* there. A sort of anti-scent, a negative. He is not alive like the girl in the woods, but not dead like the bodies in the street. He is . . .

He's like you.

The tall man looks at his hands, his arms, the black blood oozing from his calf.

This is what you are.

A moan emanates from the big man's throat, and the tall man suddenly recognizes the emotion on his face. It's the feeling of understanding a terrible truth. Of learning something that changes everything.

A piercing screech sounds from the doorway of a nearby building, and another creature emerges onto the steps above them. A female corpse, nearly as rotten as the ones in the street, her hair hanging in mangy clumps, her naked body shriveled and sagging, full of holes and tears and exposed bones.

This is what you will be.

The woman is holding something. It is an arm. A scrawny thing, black tattoos of dice and dragons and dollar bills barely visible on its brown skin, blood still trickling from its red stump. With another triumphant screech, the woman throws the arm down the stairs. It bounces and twists and lands in front of the big man, who stares at it a moment, then snatches it up and bites into its bicep.

This is what you do.

The tall man is hungry. He is so hungry. The sight of the arm has sent the brute into a frenzy, and the hollowness is so strong it's tearing him apart. The woman disappears back into the building and the tall man follows her.

The building is a coffee shop. A quaint, cozy little place lined with books, ancient bagels moldering in the pastry case, a few laptops left unattended and still not stolen. The tall man sees all this by the light of a tiny campfire in the middle of the room. A few smashed table legs stacked on a pile of crumpled book pages, burning hot and bright.

Next to the fire are two bodies. A man and a woman, one brown, one pink, one missing an arm, the other missing everything.

The tall man's mind has ceased to function. All his senses have been absorbed by the hunger. All he can see is the cloud of hands flailing in his face. All he can smell or taste or even feel is the scent. The perfume.

Life.

And all he can hear is the brute screaming at him to take it.

THIS, it bellows over and over as its myriad fingers jab at the bodies. *THIS THIS THIS.*

While the rotten woman gnaws on the brown man's thigh, the tall man kneels beside his head. Glazed eyes stare up at him, a mouth frozen open in surprise, as if gasping,

What happened? How did I get here? How could I have known that my choices mattered?

The tall man sees his hands reaching out and picking up the man's remaining arm. He feels the brute prying his mouth open and shoving his head down. He feels himself chewing. And yes, he feels relief, a warm river of energy washing over his dried-up cells and reconstituting them, pooling in his chest and inflating him like a sad, sagging party balloon. But he feels no pleasure. He wishes he could feel nothing at all. He wishes he could trade everything for information, the dullest, numbest information feelings can buy, but the trading floor is closed. He bangs on the door as he satiates himself with this person's dwindling life, but the only answer is the thin, cold voice of his own thoughts.

This is what you are and why you're here. You are not a person. You are not even a wolf. You are nothing, and no city was ever built for you.

He looks up from his meal and sees the big man watching him through the book-fire's flames. He understands that they will travel together now. They will look for other creatures like themselves and gather more and more so that they can eat more and more. And he understands that no matter how many they gather, even if they become a mob of thousands, each and every one of them will be alone.

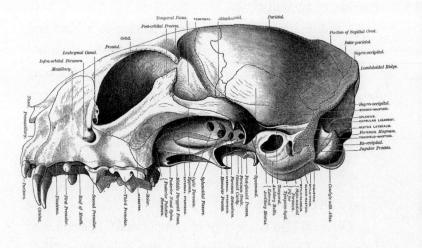

THE CARNAGE THICKENS as Nora and her brother work their way up Pine Street. The bodies are so dense she has to walk with eyes to the ground to avoid tripping over them, or worse: stepping in them. Her earlier impulse to shield Addis from the sight of death feels even more absurd now. He picks his way through the corpses with practical care, as if they're nothing more than fallen branches to be avoided. Is he indifferent to the dead? Does he make no connection between these husks and the living people he loves? Or is he simply too hungry to care?

Nora can feel her own hunger slowly consuming her loftier concerns, grinding layer after layer off the hierarchy of needs. The grand pyramid of a fully realized life eroded long ago into a practical trapezoid, and may soon collapse to the baseline of an animal.

"A police station!" Addis yelps, pointing to a blue and white building a few blocks up the hill. "Maybe there's guns!"

Nora rouses herself from her bleak forecasting and puts on a smile for her brother. "Maybe. Should we start our own police department?"

He grins.

"Want to be sheriff? I'll be your deputy."

"No, you have to start out as a regular officer and then maybe I'll promote you."

"Oh really? Do I have a lot of competition?" She points at a uniformed corpse slumped over a police motorcycle. "That guy, maybe?"

"That's . . . Sergeant Smith. He's our best guy, he'll probably beat you."

"I don't know, he looks kinda lazy."

Addis laughs.

"Sleeping on the job again, Smith?" she says in her best tough-chief growl and begins frisking the dead cop. "That's it! I want your badge on my desk, *pronto!*" She's not surprised that his gun is gone—if he still had it, why would he be dead?—but she does find a few things of interest in his pockets. Some kind of keycard and a baggie of pot. She confiscates both and they approach the station entrance.

The door is locked, which is an auspicious sign. Most easily accessed areas are stripped of anything useful. The harder a place is to reach, the more likely reaching it will be worthwhile. Nora and Addis work together to lift an empty *Seattle Times* kiosk and ram it through the tempered-glass windows.

Once inside the lobby, her hopes sink a little. The reception desk is bare and there are no posters or placards on the walls, as if the station closed down officially instead of being abandoned intact like most businesses these days. They roam through empty hallways and locker rooms, past ceramic-tiled holding cells smeared with graffiti in various mediums. The anarchy "A" drawn in blood. The Fire Church's burning Earth drawn in ash. A gigantic frown face drawn in what looks like vomit. This one strikes Nora as the most eloquent. It should replace the American flag and fly proudly over city hall, the first raw honesty to touch that place in years.

"Why didn't Dad take us here?" Addis asks as they dig through a pile of blue uniforms.

"Probably didn't know where it was."

"But he was a policeman. He should have known about it."

"He should have a lot of things."

"What if him and Mom came here? What if they took all the bullets and stuff already?"

"Addy, there are plenty of people for us to worry about without bringing Mom and Dad into it."

"No there aren't."

"Well . . . maybe not here. But other places."

"Why is everywhere always empty? Where do people go?"

"Some of them find shelter. Like skyscrapers or stadiums."

"And the other ones die, right? Like all those people out in the road?"

She pauses. "Right."

"Okay."

He finds a riot helmet and crams it down over his springy hair. "Halt!" he orders in cop-voice, and Nora smiles through a rush of bittersweet sadness that takes her a moment to understand. Nostalgia for the present. Her brother is still here, but she has already begun missing him.

"I like this place," he says. "Maybe we should stay here tonight."

Nora looks around the station, considering it. "We broke the window. Anything could come in here and get us."

"We could lock ourselves in the jail!" He starts giggling halfway through this idea.

"We need a simple building we can lock from the inside and get out of easily if we have to. This place has too many places to get trapped in. Once we're done in here, we'll go find a house."

"Aww," he says with genuine disappointment, and Nora wonders if being in the police station feels like being with his father. She wonders if he remembers the time Ababa Germame—aka Bob Greene—showed his kids around the DC precinct when Nora was twelve and Addis was three. The man was so proud. He had worked so hard, overcome such odds. None of his friends from the neighborhood could believe he had made it through the academy, even in its drastically simplified mid-apocalyptic form. Neither could his wife, who mocked and resented every forward step he took. And maybe all that doubt finally convinced him, because it was less than a year before he decided his shift would be easier with some amphetamines in his veins and shot a teenager for flipping him off, ending his brief foray into the world of unbroken people.

Nora glances over her shoulder. One dark thought leads to another and she feels shadows creeping across her back. "Wait here a second," she tells her brother. "I'm gonna go check outside."

"Why?"

"To see if those things are still following us."

"But they're slow. We can just walk away from them."

"Not if they trap us in a cramped building like this. And there might be more of them around here."

"Really?" Addis's eyes widen as if he's never considered this, which worries Nora.

"Of course, Addy, duh. What do you think ate the brains out of all those people in the street?"

"If there's more, where are they?"

"Could be anywhere. I don't think there's a hive in Seattle, so they'll just be wandering around. That's why we have to be super careful."

"Okay."

"Be right back."

She jogs out into the lobby and crawls through the shattered window. The street is still motionless, just a desolate garden of sun-wrinkled corpses. Could it be that Boney and Clyde finally gave up? Went off in search of easier heists?

She hurries back to the station locker room, but her

brother is not there. "Addis!" she shouts down the hall. She runs back into the lobby, then through the briefing room. "*Addis!*"

She finds him on the basement level, in a corner of the station they haven't yet explored.

"Look at this," he says, staring through the bars of a holding cell.

"I told you to wait," she hisses at him, but something in the way he's looking into the cell distracts her from her discipline.

"What is that?" he says, and Nora moves in behind him to see.

"Holy shit . . . ," she whispers. In the corner of the cell sits a pile of small cubes, glittering like diamonds in their foil wrappers. "I think that's . . ."

She scans the wall around the cell door, finds the lock mechanism, and slips the cop's keycard into it. The steel door unlocks with a loud *clack* and Nora heaves it open.

"What is it, what is it?" Addis demands, hopping on his toes.

Nora picks up one of the cubes and studies the wrapper. "Carbtein," she reads incredulously. "Oh my God Addy this is *Carbtein!*"

"What's Carbtein!"

"It's . . . *food*. Like . . . *super* food, for soldiers and cops and stuff. Oh my God I can't believe this."

"What's super food?"

"Here, just shut up and eat one." She tears open the wrapper and hands the white cube to Addis. He regards it skeptically.

"This is food?"

"It's like . . . concentrated food. They break stuff down to the basic nutrients and it just . . . goes right into your cells."

Addis turns the cube in his hand, grimacing. He licks it cautiously. "It's salty." He nibbles a tiny bite off the corner. "But kinda sour, too." He swallows hard, then closes his eyes and shudders. "Gross."

Nora unwraps a cube and bites it in half. It has the texture of moist chalk, like a candy Valentine heart, but its flavor is a disorienting mix of dissonant notes: sweet, sour, salty, bitter, and a few that her mind can't quite label. She concurs with her brother's review.

"This is what we're gonna eat?" Addis moans.

Nora is still chewing her first bite. The stuff resists her saliva; it won't dissolve. She keeps chewing it into smaller and smaller particles until she finally convinces her throat to swallow. She gags, but when it hits her stomach she feels something remarkable. A wave of warmth spreads out from her core like she's just taken a shot of whiskey. It will stay in her belly for hours, slowly releasing nutrients like an IV drip feed, and despite the awful taste lingering in her mouth, she smiles. Up until this moment, her plans for their future have been very small. Walk a little farther. Live a few more days. She has not allowed her mind to wander past tomorrow because tomorrow was a wall and beyond it a smothering black void she dared not approach. But a horizon has appeared.

"Eat as much as you can," she tells her brother. "If you can get that whole cube down, you won't get hungry for two or three days."

He moans again and takes a halfhearted bite.

Nora begins cramming the little foil packages into her backpack. Addis watches in dismay.

"Hey," she says. "This is the best thing that's ever happened to us."

"Is not," he mumbles.

"There's probably two hundred cubes here! We can live off this for a *year*!"

He groans.

"Oh so you'd rather starve?"

"Maybe."

She stops packing and fixes him with a hard stare. She knows he's just a seven-year-old whining about food just like any seven-year-old in any era, but she is suddenly filled with rage. "You listen to me," she says. "We are not at Auntie's house, okay? It is not your fucking birthday. We are *dying*. Do you understand that?"

Addis is quiet.

"You get a few bites to eat and you forget what starving feels like. Well I don't. It's my job to take care of you now and I'm doing the best I can, but I'm scared shitless and all I ever dream about is failing. So don't you fucking tell me you'd rather starve."

He looks at the ground. "Sorry."

"I'll let you know next time I find pizza and ice cream but for now let's just try to stay alive, okay?"

He sighs and takes another bite of his cube.

"Okay," Nora says. "Let's go find somewhere to sleep."

When they emerge from the police station the sun is

all the way down, leaving only a residual orange glow as it journeys west. Down where Pine intersects Broadway, a few street lamps flicker on. Nora sees the big man and his woman trudging steadily up the hill. And now someone else. Another man trailing an awkward distance behind them, like a surly teen who doesn't want to be seen with his parents. So they're gaining converts. Trying to start a hive. Even the Dead want a family.

Well you can't have mine, she mutters under her breath, and pulls Addis the other way.

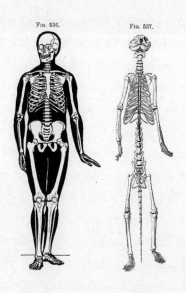

Tʜɪʀᴛʏ-ꜰᴏᴜʀ ᴍɪʟᴇꜱ ɴᴏʀᴛʜ of the police station, a young girl who recently killed a young boy is watching beige houses flicker through the headlights of her family's SUV. Her father's eyes are tight on the road, her mother's on everything around the road, pistol at the ready should anything incongruous emerge from this idyllic suburban scene. They are traveling later than they usually do, later than is safe, and the girl is glad. She hates sleeping. Not just because of the nightmares, but because everything is urgent. Because life is short. Because she feels a thousand fractures running through her, and she knows they run through the world. She is racing to find the glue.

Thirty-four miles south of this girl, a man who recently

learned he is a monster is following two other monsters up a steep hill in an empty city, because he can smell life in the distance and his purpose now is to take it. A brutish thing inside him is giggling and slavering and clutching its many hands in anticipation, overjoyed to finally be obeyed, but the man himself feels none of this. Only a coldness deep in his chest, in the organ that once pumped blood and feelings and now pumps nothing. A dull ache like a severed stump numbed in ice—what was there is gone, but it hurts. It still hurts.

And three hundred feet north of these monsters are a girl and boy who are looking for new parents. Or perhaps becoming them. Both are strong, both are super smart and super cool, and both are tiny and alone in a vast, merciless, endlessly hungry world.

All six are moving toward each other, some by accident, some by intent, and though their goals differ considerably, on this particular summer night, under this particular set of cold stars, all of them are sharing the same thought:

Find people.

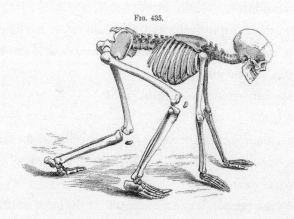

Fɪɢ. 435.

"Cᴀɴ I ɢᴇᴛ my flashlight?" Addis asks as they enter a tree-lined residential area. Nora recognizes a few of the towering mansions they saw from the highway.

"The stars are plenty bright. I don't want people seeing us."

"But I thought we're *looking* for people!"

"Not at night. Bad people come out at night."

"We're out at night."

"Okay, bad people and stupid people. But we're not looking for either of those."

He swallows hard and takes a deep breath. "I *just* swallowed the bite I took back at the police station."

"I know it's gross, Addy, but look on the bright side. You'll never have to poop."

His face freezes, then he snickers. "*What?*"

"There's zero waste in this stuff. Your body absorbs all of it. So no poop."

He laughs explosively, and Nora laughs at his laughter. "Poop," he repeats with supreme satisfaction, as if savoring a perfectly crafted joke.

"Basically what you're eating is *life*."

"What?"

"It's made out of the same stuff our cells use for energy. So it's basically human life condensed into a powder."

"We're eating *people*?"

"It's not people. It's just made out of the same stuff."

"Oh."

Nora glances over her shoulder. The street is dark except for the faint sheen of the crescent moon. She has to strain to make out the distant silhouettes stumbling along behind her. They seem to keep a steady pace at all times, and it occurs to her that if she and Addis were to sprint at full speed for as long as they could, they might be able to lose their stalkers. Except that despite being slow, the Dead have two big advantages: they can smell the Living from half a mile away, and they never have to stop. Nora realizes that sooner or later, she will have to deal with them.

"What about there?" Addis says, stopping to look at a relatively modest two-story estate. The place is an odd study in contrasts. It's an elegant, old-fashioned building, rustic red brick with white window frames and knob-topped railings on its second-floor balcony, but it has the security measures of an inner-city bank branch. Thick, wrought-iron bars on all the windows, cameras on every door, and a tall iron fence around the whole yard. The fence isn't much help due to the front gate lying flat on the ground, but still . . .

"Let's take a look," Nora says.

She pulls out her flashlight and her hatchet. Addis does the same. They begin with a quick circuit of the yard, checking the window bars, checking the doors. All intact, all locked. A convertible covered in dried blood and claw marks is the only thing out of the ordinary. In fact, the yard is oddly well kept, the shrubberies still in neat rows, the lawn weedy but not wild.

"All clear," Addis says in cop-voice.

"These window bars are pretty wide. Think you could fit?"

He tests his head against the bars. Pushing his ears flat, he could probably squeeze through. "Want me to break in?" he asks, smiling deviously. He might make a better robber than cop.

"Let's check the rest of the doors first."

They come back around to the front. Nora is surprised to find the front door—a huge, solid oak slab with reinforced hinges—unlocked. Slightly ajar. They step inside. Nora locks it behind them and clicks on her flashlight. The interior is no less luxurious than she expected. The usual exotic hardwoods and leather, paintings by real artists hanging casually in the hall.

"God," Nora whispers, aiming her flashlight at a messy, intricate collage. "That's a Rauschenberg."

"It's way too big," Addis says in a tone that means *Don't even think about it.* He remembers when the family stopped at a museum to search for weapons on dead security guards and Nora stuffed the Geo full of Picassos. He remembers when some thugs stole the car and they had to continue on foot, and she made him put all her clothes in his bag so she'd have room for some rolled-up Dali canvases. He doesn't have to worry anymore. She's much more practical these days.

They begin to explore the house. The white circles of their flashlights roam the walls like infant ghosts. Nora flicks a light switch and is surprised to see a chandelier blaze to life. She quickly switches it off.

"Why'd you turn it off?" Addis says.

"You know why."

Addis sighs. They step quietly down the hall and into the dining room. "What's that smell?" he asks, wrinkling his nose.

Nora sniffs. "Burnt plastic?" She starts to move toward the kitchen to investigate and Addis yelps, so sudden and sharp Nora almost drops her flashlight. She dashes to his side, hatchet raised. His light is creeping slowly over the faces of three corpses. Old corpses. Skeletons. No flesh but a few leathery ligaments clinging to the joints. Even their clothes have disintegrated. They recline peacefully in the living room, an adult in the easy chair and two smaller ones on the couch, their lipless mouths locked in that insane snarl that lurks behind every smile.

Addis pulls his light away and the grim tableau disappears into the shadows. He is breathing a lot harder than Nora.

"Come on," she says. "Let's check upstairs."

The top floor is just two children's bedrooms, a bathroom, and the balcony. Empty, dusty, silent.

"All clear?" Nora asks, but Addis doesn't confirm.

"Can we stay up here?" he says quietly. "We don't have to go downstairs again, do we?"

"Not if we're all clear. Are we all clear?"

"All clear."

"Okay. Then we can stay up here."

"Until it's light out?"

"Yep."

"Okay."

"Are you tired?"

"Not really."

Nora looks at his face. He is shaken. Walking over a hundred bodies rotting in the street didn't faze him, but those three skeletons seem to have reached him in a deeper place. She doubts he will sleep tonight.

"Addy," she says. "Come out on the balcony with me."

They step out into the night air and lean against the railing, looking down at the street, watching the faint moonlight shimmer on the treetops as a gentle breeze teases the leaves. Nora drops her pack at her feet—the Carbtein cubes are surprisingly heavy—and digs out her lighter, along with some shredded phone book pages she's been using for tinder. She pulls the cop's weed out of her pocket and rolls a joint. Addis watches her intently as she lights it.

"What's that stuff feel like?"

She looks at him, holding in her lungful, then breathes it out and hands him the joint.

His eyes widen. "Really?"

"Sure. It'll help you sleep."

"Mom said it's bad for kids."

"No worse than for grown-ups. Same as coffee and alcohol."

"But Mom said those are all worse for kids."

"It's not that different. Grown-ups just don't like seeing kids in altered states. It reminds them you're a person, not some little toy they sewed their faces onto."

Addis looks at her for a moment. "Are you high already?"

Nora giggles. "Maybe. I haven't smoked in a long time."

"Dad said it stunts kids' brains."

Fuck Dad, she wants to say. *Fuck them both and any advice they ever gave us. When a corpse tells you how to live, do the opposite.* Instead, she clings to her herbal calm and says, "Oh well. None of us are gonna grow up to be doctors anyway."

Addis studies the joint. He puts it to his lips and takes a dainty puff. He coughs and hands it back to her, then stares at the trees for a minute.

A slow smile creeps across his face. "Whoa . . ."

Nora sucks in another hit and they both regard the moonlit sea of trees, rooftops poking through like distant islands. She is in love with this moment. She glances at her brother, hoping to see that dopey grin again and maybe find out what stoned-child philosophy sounds like, but the grin is gone. His face has turned abruptly blank, and Nora feels a spike of dread piercing her cloud of well-being.

"Mom and Dad left us alone," he says.

Nora releases the smoke in her lungs in a long sigh.

"They were supposed to take care of us. Why did they leave?"

So soon. She thought she'd have another year to prepare for this. She looks out at the trees and auditions lies in her head.

Maybe they went to find food and got lost.

Maybe they got bitten and didn't want to infect us.

I don't know why they left.

But she rejects these. Addis deserves truth. He is a child, but why does that make him any less deserving? Nora herself is a child; so are her parents—everyone is equally young and foolish in the wide lens of history, and the arrogant denial of this is what unraveled the world. So much easier to think of people as children when you want to lie to them. Especially if you're a businessman, a congressman, a journalist, a doctor, a preacher, a teacher, or the head of a global superpower. Enough white lies can scorch the earth black.

"Addis," she says, looking her brother in the eyes. "Mom and Dad left because they couldn't take care of us. It was hard to find enough food and they wanted drugs and we were slowing them down, so they left."

Addis stares at her. "Didn't they care what happened to us?"

"Maybe they cared a lot. Maybe they were really sad about it."

"But they still did it."

"Yeah."

"They left 'cause they cared more about food and drugs than us. 'Cause staying with us was hard."

Nora winces a little but doesn't back down. "Well . . . yeah. Pretty much."

Addis looks at the ground, his face slowly tensing into a scowl. "Mom and Dad are bad people."

She begins to worry. Is this right? Should a seven-year-old be swallowing a truth this jagged?

"Good people care more about people than food," he mutters. "They try to help people and don't give up even when they get hungry." There's a strange intensity in his voice. His child falsetto sounds lower, rougher. "Only bad people give up."

"Addis . . . ," she says uneasily. "Mom and Dad are fucked-up and selfish but they're not 'bad people.' There's kinda no such thing as 'good' or 'bad' people, there's just like . . . humanity. And it gets broken sometimes."

"But good people fix things. Good people stay good even when it's hard to." He is gripping the railing so tightly his knuckles have turned white. His face is filling with a rage Nora has never seen before. "Even if they're sick or sad or they have to lose their favorite stuff. Even if they have to die."

"Addis—"

"Good people see past their own fucking lives."

Nora freezes and her eyes go wide. The air around her feels strange.

"They aren't just hunger and math. They aren't just animals."

She grabs her brother's shoulder and tries to pull him away from the railing but his muscles are stiff as wood.

"Good people are part of the Higher," he says in that deep growl, and for a brief moment, Nora swears the color of his eyes is changing. "Good people are fuel for the sun."

"Addis!" she shrieks and shakes him hard.

He turns and frowns at her. "What?"

His eyes are brown. His voice is mousy. The faint rustle of wind in the trees reclaims the night, muffled by the blood throbbing in her ears.

"What . . . what were you just saying?"

He turns his sullen gaze back to the moon. "Mom and Dad are mean."

Nora stares at the joint in her fingers. Addis reaches for it and she reflexively flicks it off the balcony.

"Why'd you *do* that?" he whines, frowning at her. "It made me feel really good."

"I don't think it's . . ." She's too rattled to finish. She shakes her head. "No more."

"Fine."

They both study the moon, Addis pouting, Nora wondering where the cop got this baggie and if perhaps there were a few other spices mixed into those herbs. That sensation of charged air is gone now, leaving only the familiar fog of a standard high. She settles into it, trying to erase the image of her brother's eyes flashing like two gold rings in the moonlight.

She aims her flashlight at the moon. She imagines her beam touching its powdery deserts and takes some whimsical comfort from the thought. A small taste of escape from this awful place. Then she swings the light back to Earth, and it glints off the silver eyes of a rotting bald giant.

She manages not to drop the flashlight and stifles most of her scream. The man is standing in the middle of the yard looking dumbly up at her, his eyes unsquinting in the flash-light's beam.

"I told you to leave us alone," she says in a shaky whisper.

The man makes no response. Just stares. He has barely rotted at all since his death. He is grey all over, but the only other sign of decay is his lips, which have gone from full and sensuous to blue and slightly shriveled. It's a shame. They were his best feature.

"Nora?" Addis says, his eyes wide with fear.

"It's okay," she says, scanning the yard with her flashlight and running mental checks on all the doors. "We're safe up here." She shines the light back into the big man's eyes like a cop interrogating a suspect. "Where's the new guy?" she yells at him in her best cop-voice, trying to force some steel into her nerves.

The man looks over his shoulder; Nora follows his gaze with her light and notices the top of a head peeking over the wall of shrubbery that surrounds the fence. She can't help a little chuckle.

"What's with him? Shy?"

"Nora . . . ," Addis whimpers, tugging on her shirt.

"I told you it's okay, Addy, they can't get up here. Hey," she calls to the big man. "Where's your girlfriend?"

He raises his arm and points at the sky.

Nora looks up, frowns, looks back at him. "What's that mean?"

He continues to point.

"She's flying?"

He lowers his arm, raises it again.

"Maybe he means she went to Heaven," Addis offers.

"Do you mean she died?" Nora asks the man.

He lowers his arm and makes no further comment.

"Well hey, I'm real sorry for your loss, but go the fuck away. We're not letting you eat us."

He doesn't respond for a moment, then a low moan rises in his throat. The tone is unmistakably mournful, so resonant with despair it makes Nora shiver. When she shines her light into his eyes she sees pain, and it disturbs her in a way she can't explain. She feels an urge to *comfort* him. She remembers all the pamphlets she's read, the stories on the news and the warnings from her parents telling her what these creatures are. The tests done on them, declaring them nothing more than corpses experiencing bizarrely prolonged death spasms. But looking into this corpse's eyes, she can see that there's a man in there. And he's suffering.

She sighs and folds her arms, turning to her brother. "What are we gonna do with these guys?"

"Shouldn't we kill them? What if they get in?"

"This place is a fortress, Addy. They can't get in."

"What if they climb up here?"

"Zombies can't climb. They have a hard enough time walking."

"Okay."

"We've got to figure something out, though. They'll still be there in the morning."

The big man waits patiently. Nora can hear the new guy pacing anxiously behind the hedge.

"They're probably just hungry, right?" Addis says. "That one was trying to eat that wolf."

"They're always hungry. But they have to eat people; animal energy doesn't work. Maybe he hasn't figured that out yet."

"What about Carbtein?"

"What about it?"

"You said it was like life powder."

Nora's eyes drift. "Right . . ."

"So maybe we could feed some to them? And they'd get full and leave us alone?"

"Addis Horace Greene," she says in a tone of pleasant surprise. "You *are* super smart."

He grins.

"Let's try it. Toss him one."

Addis pulls a cube out of the backpack and unwraps it. "Hey!" he calls down to the man. "Eat this and leave us alone!" He throws the cube. It hits the man directly in the face. The man backs away, looking up at them in surprise.

Nora giggles. "That's *food*, dumb-ass!" she says, pointing down to where the cube fell. "It's human energy! You can eat it."

He looks down at the cube. He looks up at Nora. He picks up the cube, sniffs it, and stuffs the entire thing in his mouth.

Addis laughs. "He likes it!"

Nora watches him chew. "This could be a big deal, Addy. They could put piles of it all over the city and keep the zombies fed. Then maybe they wouldn't—"

The man spits out his mouthful in a gooey pile of white shards, then stares up at Nora as if waiting for more.

"What the fuck, man?" She pulls another cube out of her backpack and rubs it hard against her wrist, leaving red abrasions caked with white powder. "*Swallow* it!" She raises it over her head to throw. "It's human life, it's what you—"

Something clamps onto her wrist. A withered vise of leather and bone—a hand, but barely. She looks up into a face but finds no eyes, just gluey blobs stuck to the sides of empty sockets. A skeleton shrink-wrapped in flesh is crouching at the edge of the roof like a spider, bracing against the gutter with one hand and gripping Nora's with the other. Only the tendrils of blond hair dangling from its scalp tell her this was once a human woman. A warbling hum emanates from its bones.

Nora buckles her knees and yanks against the thing's grip but it's shockingly strong—her knees dangle above the balcony floor with her full weight grinding against her wrist. The creature bites the Carbtein cube out of her hand and chews briefly, then tilts its head and lets the chunks drop out in strings of brown saliva. It looks at the man far below on the ground. It looks at Nora. It shoves her hand in its mouth and bites off her ring finger.

What happens then happens so fast it barely reaches Nora's brain: blurry, disjointed images in flickery black and white. Before the pain in her finger even registers, her brother is standing in front of her and jumping up and swinging his hatchet; the creature's arm snaps off above the wrist. He is yanking her back into the house and slamming the balcony door and slapping her hand down on the floor and then he is spreading her fingers away from her ring finger and swinging his hatchet down hard. The remainder of her finger jumps away from her hand and rolls into one of the children's rooms. She stares at it, and when the hoarse scream rises in her throat, she's not sure if it's from the pain—a deep, aching agony that radiates through her hand and up into her arm— or from watching her severed finger turn grey, black, then shrivel up and slough away to bone right there in front of her.

"I'm sorry I'm sorry!" Addis is sobbing as he inches away from the blood pooling under Nora's hand. She wants to tell him it's okay; she wants to thank him and tell him she loves him so much, but she can see the creature through the balcony door's windows, crouched on all fours and tearing apart her backpack, crunching greedy mouthfuls of Carbtein and drooling it back out in slimy piles. *"Why?"* she screams hysterically at the door, watching her and her brother's future disappear into the thing's gnarled jaws. The thing just glances at her briefly and keeps chewing, and Nora feels her mind sinking into a dark well.

She wobbles to her feet, squeezing her left wrist tight with her right hand. "Come on," she hisses and staggers down the staircase. When she hits the bottom she pauses to listen. No breaking glass. No crunching wood. Even the sound of the thing's frenzied chewing has stopped, and the house is silent. Where did it go? Surely one knuckle wasn't enough to satisfy its hunger. That little nibble of finger food?

An unhinged giggle escapes her throat. Her head is swimming.

Addis dashes down hallways and sweeps his flashlight over doors and windows, checking the perimeter, but the house is still empty except for the family of skeletons reclining in the living room. Their yellowed faces sneer at Nora as Addis passes his light over them, casting all their awful edges in sharp relief.

She smells that burnt odor again. Plastic? Hair?

"Nora?" Addis whispers.

She sees a wisp of smoke pass through his beam and glances around in the dark.

"These skeletons . . . how come their skulls aren't open like the ones in the street?"

Nora freezes. She follows her brother's flashlight beam to where it rests on the father's cranium. And she notices—no cracks. No bullet holes. No gaping lobotomy. Inside that skull is an intact brain.

This is when she hears a noise, but not from upstairs. From the kitchen. A dry scraping, then the metallic squeak of an oven door opening.

Nora turns around. A skeleton is straightening up from behind the oven, holding a smoking baking pan in its bare bone hands. The pan's Teflon peels off the sides in smoldering flakes. The skeleton carries the pan into the dining room and sets it on the table, where it sizzles on the cherrywood, adding more bitter smoke to the already acrid air. The skeleton is wearing an apron. Bits of long hair cling to its thin film of a scalp. The baking pan is empty.

The father rises from its easy chair in a noisy clatter of bones. The two children follow. They all sit at the dining table and begin dipping forks into the empty pan, serving nothing onto their white china plates, shoveling nothing into their mouths, teeth scraping and grinding on the steel tines. Then in mid-bite, as if surprised by a dinnertime doorbell, they all pause in unison and turn their heads to look at Nora.

Addis is the first to scream. Nora grabs his hand, ignoring the pain in her finger stump, and rushes to the front door. She is reaching for the latch when she sees two decomposing faces peering through the door's window. She whirls around to head for the back door but the skeletal family is lined up at the end of the hall, staring with those grotesquely cheerful grins. The front door rattles violently. The big man is trying to force his way in. Nora has a flash of irrational hope, imagining for a moment that he is coming to save her, but then his fist smashes through the door's window and she sees the look on his face, no longer pain but pure, mindless hunger. Whatever she saw in him before is rapidly departing.

The man and his partner are at the front door and the family is planted at the end of the hall, clawlike fingers twitching and pinching the air. There is no exit.

Nora pulls Addis into the hallway half-bathroom, a tiny box containing only a sink, a toilet, and a narrow window looking into the side yard. The room is barely wide enough for two people abreast. A good enough place for a last stand.

"Stay behind me," she whispers. "If they get me . . ." She doesn't finish. There is nothing else to say.

She holds her breath and listens. Louder than anything she hears her heart pummeling her breastbone. Throbbing in her temples and roaring in her ears. The tiny howls of her finger nerves, reaching out into open space and grasping around for their cut endings.

The big man has stopped pounding the door. There is silence in the hall. Then footsteps. Slow, one at a time, bone feet tapping the hardwood like dog claws or stiletto heels. The click of a latch. Squeak of a door. More footsteps, much heavier, but softened by shoes. Then silence.

Nora tenses. She grips the hatchet in both hands despite the growing numbness in her right. Addis is huddled behind her on the toilet seat, breathing hard but too terrified to cry. Her wide stance fills the room's width, shielding him. She indulges in one selfish thought: if he dies, at least she won't be here to see it. She is his big sister. She gets to go first.

She glances back to tell him she loves him. The woman's shriveled face is grinning in the window. A spear of bone punches through the glass and through Addis. The spear lifts him, a hand grabs him, and he disappears through the window hole.

Nora is alone in the bathroom, staring into a dark yard of neat grass and trimmed shrubberies, just her and the soft chirp of crickets.

Her face contorts and trembles in a soundless shriek. She kicks open the bathroom door. The hall is empty. She runs through the wide-open front door and dashes around the house, waving her flashlight in wild arcs. She sees the back door swinging open and staggers back inside.

Everyone has gathered in the living room. The big man and the woman are kneeling on the floor in front of the coffee table. Addis lies on its ornate oak slab, his blood pooling in the engraved flowers and paisleys. The man and the woman gaze down on him and the skeletons lean in eagerly, angels in a satanic nativity.

Addis looks at Nora. He says something but it's too faint. The big man scoops him up in his powerful arms and rises to his feet. The man looks at Nora. The spark of awareness is still there, weakened and faded, but there, and so is the pain. Then the woman thing stands up and touches his arm. Its sharp fingers press until they break his skin. Nora hears that warbling hum rising in the room, vibrating from within the creature and all the skeletons too, a thick and dissonant chord like a hundred cracked wineglasses singing in unison.

Over the top of this noise, the creature speaks. Its jaw opens and a dry, rasping caw emerges, shrill and cruel, full of wordless rage bubbling up and blaring like a dictator's megaphone into the man's ear.

The man's eyes change. His brows and lips go slack. His pain and longing and uncertainty go away.

"No," Nora croaks. *"No!"*

The man bites into Addis's shoulder. Addis begins to shake.

Nora clamps her eyes shut so hard it hurts. She runs backward, she bumps into a chair then a wall then stumbles out onto the lawn. All she sees is blackness and sparks but in her mind the house is crumbling, brick disintegrating, walls toppling in on themselves and then a black cloud of dust that chokes the air and hides everything, erases everything, makes everything gone.

She grips her face in her hands, squeezing out all thought.

No.

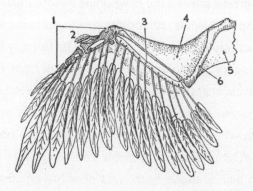

Julie's eyes open halfway. Morning sun refracts through the water in them, making abstract art in her lashes and salts. She has just woken from a long night of dreams, bad like they always are now. She dreamt she was a monster. She dreamt she was alone in an empty school. She dreamt a skeleton had stolen her mother's white dress and was dancing on a roof with her father.

She feels a rumbling under her and realizes the truck is moving. She sits up and wipes the crust out of her eyes. The sun has the shy, tentative angle of early dawn.

"Mom?" she says, and her mother's eyes appear in the mirror, blue like hers but paler.

"Hi, honey," she says.

Julie stretches her limbs. "Where are we?"

"Just coming up on Seattle. See?"

They crest a hill and the city skyline sweeps into view. She sees the Space Needle, still pointing straight and true, lights blinking calmly like nothing is wrong. The freeway begins to congest as they get closer to downtown. A permanent traffic jam of derelict cars crashed or abandoned in the street. Julie's father slows to weave through the mess, carefully bulldozing cars aside when necessary. Julie keeps her eyes on the sky to avoid seeing whatever is inside those cars. She feels too fragile to take in more death right now. She is already filled to the brim.

This upward gaze is why, as they approach an overpass, she notices a girl stumbling across it.

"Dad!" she shouts and points wildly. "Look!"

"Oh God . . . ," her mother whispers.

Her father stops the truck but says nothing. They all watch the girl make her way toward the other side of the freeway. Slow, shuffling steps. Empty, dull-eyed stare. A blood-smeared hand with a missing finger swinging against her hip.

Julie's father looks back at the road and drives forward.

"Dad!"

"She's Dead."

"We don't know that," Audrey says.

"You saw how she's walking. You saw her hand. Alone in an exed city without even a backpack? She's Dead."

"What if she's just hurt?" Julie demands.

"It's clearly a bite. If she hasn't converted yet, she will in a few minutes."

Julie cranes her neck to look back at the overpass. "Dad, we have to at least check!"

"What's the point, Julie?" For the first time this morning his eyes appear in the mirror, and Julie glimpses pain in them. "Do you want to make another new friend just to watch her become a corpse? Are you going to shoot her or will I have to?"

Julie's eyes sting and her mouth trembles. She looks at the girl, older than her, older than the boy she killed yesterday, maybe closer to Nikki's age, walking alone on a bridge.

She opens the truck's door and jumps out.

The truck is not moving fast but the pavement sweeps her feet out from under her and she falls, lands on her elbows and then her mouth; she feels a few teeth loosen. Heedless of the salty flood pouring down her throat, she scrambles to her feet and runs toward the overpass, screaming, "Hey! Hey!"

The girl on the overpass doesn't seem to hear her. She continues stumbling forward.

"You're not Dead!" Julie chokes through her tears. "You're *not* Dead! You can come with us!"

Steely arms wrap around her from behind and pull her off her feet. *"Julie,"* her father hisses. "Jesus Christ, Julie."

She collapses into her father's grip, sobbing uncontrollably as blood streams down her chin and onto her T-shirt. She feels the cracks in the world widening. She feels it breaking.

Her father looks up at the girl on the overpass. "Ma'am?"

he shouts like a weary cop reciting procedure. "Have you been bitten?"

The girl stares at him.

"Are you infected?"

She wobbles on her feet and says nothing.

Julie's father scans the streets leading to the overpass, sizing up the risk and difficulty of reaching the girl, and shakes his head. He pulls Julie back toward the truck.

Julie tries to fight him but her body has gone limp. She feels his logic tugging at her brain but she fights that, too. His logic is sound. He's not incorrect. But he's wrong.

"Follow us!" Julie shouts hoarsely.

The girl on the overpass finally looks at her. Her gaze is unsteady, but so is Julie's, blurred by hot streams of tears.

"We're going to South Cascadia! There's a stadium with people in it!"

Her father shoves her into the truck and slams the door. She rolls down the window and sticks her head out. "If you're not Dead, come south! Meet us there!"

Without a word or a pause her father starts driving, resuming their slow crawl through traffic as if nothing has happened, but his face is harder than she has ever seen it. Her mother reaches back and dabs at her chin with a rag, soaking up the pink mixture of blood and tears. Julie's eyes lock with hers, pleading for something she can't articulate. Her mother's lips tremble briefly, then they stiffen. She breaks away from Julie's gaze.

"Your teeth might end up a little crooked," she says, staring straight ahead. "But you'll be okay. We'll bandage your elbows at the next safe stop." The Tahoe grinds against a rusted convertible and pushes it out of the way. A man-sized pile of rags crunches under the tires. "John, stop at the next department store, please."

"Why?"

Julie leans forward to find her mother's face in the mirror, but all she can see is the white dress, her mother's fingers tugging at the holes.

"I need some real clothes."

The sky is a pale, dry blue like it always is now, even on perfect, cloudless afternoons. Smog, dust, airborne radiation; Julie doesn't know what it is. But from old photos she knows the blue was deeper, once. Her father tells her it's just a trick of photography, but she doesn't believe him. She sees it in her dreams. Even when they're nightmares.

Julie has had many nightmares in her short life. She is twelve, but she has seen death from more angles than her grandfather did in forty years of military service. She will grow up quickly. She will harden in places she shouldn't and break apart in others, and she will bury both her parents before she's old enough to buy beer. But even now she knows: this is living. She won't object to it or call it unfair, even though it is very, very unfair. Life is only fair for the Dead, who get what they want because they want nothing. Julie wants everything, no matter how much it costs, and this is why she will change the world.

She watches the girl on the overpass shrinking into the distance. Their eyes meet across a river of cars. Just before the girl disappears, Julie drops something out the window.

• • •

"You're not dead!"

The tall man watches the short girl stumble toward him on the street below, blood trickling down her chin and arms, bright red instead of black because she is alive. The brute is screaming again because there is another Living girl even closer to him, this one tall with black hair and brown skin and life that smells like liquor. The brute wants to take it and drink it, but the tall man is not moving. He hides behind a rusty truck, peering through its windows at the mystery unfolding in front of him. The tall girl is only a few yards away, but he ignores the commands throbbing in his hands and teeth and just watches the tiny blond creature below.

She spits a mouthful of blood onto the asphalt and sucks in a lungful of air. "You're not dead!" she shouts in a voice so very different from the melodic tones he heard in the forest yet in its own way beautiful, a broken sound of grief and desperate hope. Somehow these emotions ring clear to him despite his growing inability to feel them, and he wonders with some amazement why the girl is talking to him.

"Dead . . . ," he croaks, slowly molding his tongue into the necessary shapes.

"You're *not* dead!"

His eyes widen. He is more confused now than when he woke up near a river with a mind as dark as deep space. What does she mean? What is she trying to tell him? He knows he is not alive. If he were alive, everything would be different. If he were alive he would be sitting on a park bench with a mug of hot coffee reading his favorite book for the fifth or tenth time, glancing up now and then to watch the people stroll by, and the city would smile and lean in and whisper: *That bench was shaped for your body. That book was written for your mind. This city was built for your life, and all these people were born to share it with you. You are part of this, living man. Go live.*

If he were alive, he would not be walking through a concrete graveyard with a crowd of corpses, looking for lives to erase.

So why does this girl insist he's not dead? He knows she is wiser than him. He heard it in her singing. Can he somehow believe her? He is not alive, that much is clear, but he *is* walking. He *does* have eyes, unlike the big man's shriveled girlfriend, who is barely distinguishable from all the person-shaped piles littering the streets. He hasn't fully surrendered to rot.

"Not . . . dead?" he murmurs, pressing his face against the truck's grimy glass.

"You can come with us!"

The girl's father has her now, dragging her away, and the tall man feels a sting in his eyes. After all this time and all the things he's given up, it seems there are still things he wants. The brute tries relentlessly to shove them aside, hammering down every desire that isn't hunger, but they remain. And he finds, to his surprise, that he wants them to.

Behind him, he hears the scraping of dry bone on pavement. He leaves the tall girl on the bridge and intercepts the others as they emerge from an alleyway. The big man, the small boy, and five creaking skeletons, their withered bones humming with the strange darkness that drives them. They would have killed the boy. They would have gleefully devoured his brain, a tiny sun hot and dense with life. But they restrained themselves for one simple reason: they need him to help kill others. They need to grow their terrible family, to add more teeth to their mouth so that it can eat the world.

As they sniff the air in the direction of the overpass, the tall man feels something move inside him.

It is not the brute.

"Guns," he wheezes.

They regard him blankly.

"Too . . . many guns."

He starts walking away from the overpass and after a brief hesitation, dazzled by the decisiveness of his movements, the others follow him.

The big man walks alongside him, giving him a curious look. The tall man returns it, unblinking.

"Name?" he wheezes at the big man.

The big man considers this with a troubled expression, as if he's been asked to do something unnatural. Finally, a hum builds between his lips. "Mmmm."

The tall man nods. "Rrrrr."

The big man nods. They keep walking.

They walk away from the tall girl on the bridge, away from the short girl and her family disappearing into the distance, away from this beautiful city and its silent condemnation. The tall man doesn't know where they're going and doesn't care. He is spent. His mind is mercury again, its brief surge of humanity melting into an oily residue on its surface, and he no longer understands the feelings he felt in that strange moment on the overpass.

But he did feel them. They did happen. They rest on the murky seabed of his mind, buried under sand and silt and miles of grey waves, patient seeds waiting for light.

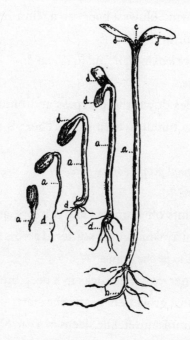

"Y̶ou're not Dead!"

Nora watches the apparition move toward her on the street below. Golden hair, azure eyes, fair skin like the saints on her mother's candles, except those saints never had blood running down their chins.

"We're going to South Cascadia!"

The apparition is moving away now, getting smaller.

"You're not Dead! You can come with us!"

Nora blinks, and the apparition is gone. She is alone on a bridge, overlooking miles of desolation. She stands there for a while, watching the apparition's truck disappear into the distance. The wind blows a beer can against her feet, bits of ash into her hair.

"What are we looking for?" Addis demands.

"Good people."

She stumbles down the overpass and onto the freeway, walks for a few minutes, then stops. There is something on the road.

"There are good people somewhere."

"Are you sure?"

The sun glints off bumpers and mirrors, and off the foil wrappers of thirty small cubes scattered across the pavement.

"There's got to be one or two."

She closes her eyes. She sucks in a deep breath. She gathers the cubes in a grocery bag, and she starts walking.

She walks until sunset. She sleeps in a car. She wakes up at sunrise and starts walking again. She thinks about the volleyball. Its smooth white simplicity; bump, set, spike. One clear thought to keep aloft, nothing more, and now her volleyball is this: to become a good person. To make her brother proud of her. And to find a way to save him.

So Nora Aynalem Greene is walking. She is sixteen years old, but now she is seventeen. Now she is twenty-four. She is seeking a cure for the plague, the curse, the judgment—people may never agree on what to call it. She will search for years until she forgets this city and its horrors, until she forgets she ever had a family and begins to think of herself as something that sprouted unbidden and unwanted through the concrete of an empty parking lot. But even then, alone in the driest desert, she knows that a rain will fall. It may be a long time, but not forever. Nora knows better than most that nothing lasts forever. Life doesn't, love doesn't, hope doesn't, so why would death or hate or despair?

Nothing is permanent. Not even the end of the world.

end

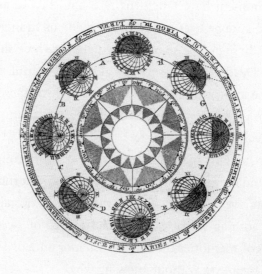

This is not the end.

The end is darkness and fire. Madness and war. A quiet retreat into extinction on a drained and barren Earth. The end is the dissolution of all bonds and the dissipation of all warmth, the scattering of all hearts across the desert of the world.

This is not the end. We are not standing on that howling ledge. As dim as our skies are, as far off as we've wandered, we have not yet reached that hopeless place, and sometimes we dream that we won't.

What if entropy is a puzzle that life can solve? What if the Library has no ceiling and the ladder goes up and up?

We don't often indulge in such wild fantasies. Eons of disappointment have taught us restraint. But we are reading these strange lives and they are giving us strange hopes, because these people shouldn't be here. All three should be dead or Dead or at the very least broken—fearful, distrustful, alone in their despair. But they are none of these things. They are alive and together on the roof of a stadium, waiting patiently for the sun.

Our thoughts bleed into theirs as we flip through their books, and they shiver. They chalk it up to the morning wind whipping over the roof. They write it off as nostalgia, but we are nothing so cheap. They feel a swell of sweet grief, outlines of memories they've forgotten or buried. They find tears in their eyes without knowing why.

We know their names now. Who they were and who they are, and who they hope to be. They huddle together on the blanket, three human beings out of the half-starved hundred million remaining on the earth, and though they have only faint suspicions that we exist, we sit close to them like friends—like family—willing them to feel our warmth.

We are almost full. We are near the brim. Soon we'll spill over and everything will change, but not this morning. Earth has a few more revolutions to make.

ACKNOWLEDGMENTS

Thanks to my parents for trusting me when I say this isn't about them. Thanks to my brother, Nathan, for all the support and prodding, and to my sister, Nurse Christa, for all the medical info. Thanks to Joe Regal, Markus Hoffmann, Emily Bestler, and everyone else who helped this book exist. Thanks to everyone involved in the movie, for making people care that this book exists. Thanks to the kids I met while working in the foster care system, for showing me what badasses look like.

A hard climb toward humanity. A past life
that won't stay buried. And a rising threat so insidious,
even the Dead are on its payroll.

R's journey continues into the beautiful,
terrible world of . . .

THE LIVING

Turn the page for an excerpt.

THERE HAS NEVER BEEN a more efficient departure in the history of commercial air travel. The moment I lock the door behind me the plane shudders away from the gate. No searching for seats, no wrestling with the overhead bins, and certainly no safety demonstration. While I lock my kids in the bathroom—they seemed comfortable enough when I found them there—Abram taxis onto the runway like the two-hundred-foot plane is a sports car. The black specks behind us have grown into black lumps. Their warbling drone fills my ears like angry bees. I almost tumble down the aisle when Abram guns the engines and the plane surges forward.

"R!" Julie calls to me from business class. "Get up here!"

I fight my way forward while inertia drags me back. By the time I reach Julie, the plane is shuddering and shaking like we're driving on a country road.

"Marcus!" Abram calls back to M, who's sitting in the back of business class, several seats removed from the rest of us. "You cleared the runway, right?"

"Yes," M says through gritted teeth, gripping the armrests so tight his fingers tremble.

Nora smiles at him. "Scared of flying?"

His eyes are wide. Beads of sweat glisten on his forehead. "Little bit."

"I've never flown before. I'm excited."

"Happy for you," he growls, and Nora laughs. She reaches over and puts a hand on his forearm.

"Marcus. After everything we've lived through, there is no way we're gonna die in a damn plane crash. God isn't witty enough for a joke that good."

M takes a deep breath and lets it out slowly. Nora pats his arm and settles back into her seat.

I fall into mine next to Julie and brace myself as the plane threatens to tear itself apart. She reaches out and grabs my hand, and I see no fear in her eyes. Despite everything, despite the many possible deaths circling our heads at this moment, the rattling of the plane and the choppers behind it and the unknown wilderness we're flying into, her eyes are full of hope. It's so bright that for a moment I swear there's a glimmer of gold in their icy blue.

"Here we go," she says, and with a final lunge, the plane leaves the ground. The shuddering stops. The only sound is the engines. We are gliding through space.

"Wow," I hear Abram gasp to no one in particular, and I realize how little he actually expected this to work.

I scan the windows behind me until I find our pursuers. They are plainly visible now, but they have stopped growing. If they were equipped with rockets or even high-caliber guns like the last one, we might be in trouble, but these are not gunships. They are light craft salvaged from news stations and corporate buildings, and as we climb rapidly and they shrink away beneath us, the distant flashes of their rifles and handguns become less and less frightening. Finally, a towering cumulus welcomes us into its cottony bosom, and the world goes white.

A tightly held breath bursts out of M in the form of incredulous laughter.

Nora stares out the window, awestruck.

From the cockpit, I hear Sprout giggling and clapping in the co-pilot's chair.

Julie squeezes my hand, and I realize it's her left hand. Either she's ignoring the pain in her finger, or she's forgotten it.

The fog around us flickers a few times, and suddenly we're above it. An impossible fantasy landscape of creamy white towers stretches out before us, and here and there, through holes and gaps, the real world peeks through below, full of unknown threats and promises, shouting at us to come back down and fight.

We're coming, I tell the world, squeezing Julie's hand harder. *We're ready for you.*